THE SMELL OF VANILLA WOODEN SCREENS

Frank G Schafer

© 2017 Frank G Schafer
All rights reserved.

ISBN: 1974135284
ISBN 13: 9781974135288

These two stories are a work of fiction. Any references to real people, events, quotations, establishments, organizations, or locale are intended only to give the fiction a sense of reality and authenticity and are used fictitiously. All other names, characters, and places and all dialogue and incidents portrayed in these stories are the product of the authors imagination.

CONTENTS

The Smell of Vanilla   1
Wooden Screens   26

I was recently introduced to the writings of Charles Bukowski

Someone should make a movie about his life.

Charles Bukowski quotes:

"I kept writing not because I felt I was good, but because I felt they were so bad including Shakespeare, all those, like chewing cardboard."

"I don't like jail, they got the wrong kind of bars in there."

"An intellectual says a simple thing a hard way. An artist says a hard thing in a simple way."

"Sometimes I've called writing a disease. If so, I'm glad it caught me."

As usual, I thank Linda (The Acorn)

    She stands by me, solid, like an oak tree

I also thank my local editors J. II, and a couple of others, they know who they are.

THE SMELL OF VANILLA

As donated livers go, this one looked quite ordinary, certainly healthy, especially as compared to the gray craggy looking organ that the surgeon, Dr. Timothy Cutter, was removing from Gabriel's upper abdomen. He remarked to the attending physician, Dr. Remy Remuva, that he had never seen such a wretched liver in a living person. He further stated that the patient was lucky indeed, as he doubted he would have lived another day.

A short time later, Dr. Cutter's work was done, and he left the room as Dr. Remuva took the stapling gun from the nurse's tray.

Gabriel was most likely the sickest of the sick in St Peter's Hospital of Angels on that bleak morning in early February 2015. Jeremy (clad in mask and gown) was waiting patiently in the private intensive care room for them to bring his soul mate back from recovery.

Doctor Cutter had already informed him that the liver transplant had been successful, and now Gabriel's fate was in the hands of the angels, as he so often said to loved ones and relatives after the surgeries he performed.

They wheeled Gabriel in. A dozen tubes coming in and out of his torso would be a conservative number. He lay there motionless, except for the small, almost imperceptible, rise and fall of his now frail chest. Jeremy allowed for a nostalgic image to enter his mind.

He remembered the first night he met his true love. It was at a party thrown by a good friend, the famous Lebanese choreographer, Suq Madiq, to celebrate the closing of one of the longest runs of any Broadway musical ever, the internationally famous, *The Sound of Orgasm*. This show boasted an all LGBT troop. These beautiful people danced and sung their way into the hearts of all the folks who stood in long lines to see them. But the most perfect and beautiful one of all was the star, Gabriel.

Gabriel was stunning to look at; six feet exactly, with blue black hair, gelled and combed back tight to his head. He had thick black eyebrows that sat above all knowing, azure blue eyes. His eyelashes were natural and ridiculously long, with tattooed eyeliner to boot. He was dressed to the nines as usual. This night, he was resplendent in white. White penny loafers, no socks of course, white, tight, no belt slacks that were very revealing, obviously showcasing what he liked to call, his camel hump. On the top, he wore a white silk transparent blouse, mostly unbuttoned, revealing the thick black hair of his chest that was not unlike that of a living wild animal just resting there, and of course, in his hand, a mint julep, his favorite.

Jeremy had seen the musical many times and was certainly awed by the man. But to see him up close in person was like being in the presence of Jesus. He could feel his pulse quicken as well as that familiar burn in his groin at the sight of him.

Gabriel was playing the room like a politician. When he was introduced to Jeremy, he stopped in his tracks; his gay-dar was fully on. He said, "Well hello there, gorgeous, let me ask you a question? What has 142 teeth and holds back the Incredible Hulk?" Jeremy was taken by surprise by this unexpected attention, and could only hesitantly answer, "Wh, what?"

"My zipper!" All those in ear shot laughed heartily, as they always did in the star's presence. Jeremy, still befuddled, did not know quite how to react. He just sort of sounded out a whispered chortle, for he had not yet come out, and he was still resistant to the idea of it. He was gay of course, and had a few encounters, but he was still keeping his gayness on the down- low. A family consideration was the excuse he used. He was now nearly twenty-nine and frankly, tired of the ruse. He knew he would soon blow the lid off it, no matter what the consequences.

Jeremy watched closely as Gabriel pranced about the room. Soon he worked his way back to him. He managed to get behind Jeremy and whisper in his ear. He said, "I know you're still hiding. That really turns me on. Meet me at my car in the parking garage on level two in ten minutes. Just look for the red Porsche Carrera near the elevator."

Panic set in. This whisper was so unexpected. He had pleasured himself so many nights with thoughts of being with Gabriel that he was beside himself with anxiety. Would he dare to be so brave? Should he take the chance that he might be just another conquest of the more-than-famous libido of this star? Two minutes of thought was all it took. He would rendezvous with him as he was told.

It was twenty degrees and windy on this cold February night. He spent nearly thirty minutes leaning against the concrete wall of the parking garage. He found a spot just out of the light. He was about to call it quits, when the elevator door opened and out came Gabriel, dancing and singing a perfect rendition of Rod Stewart's, "Tonight's the Night". He spotted Jeremy. He danced over to him still singing beautifully and when he got next to him he kissed him hotly on the mouth. With that kiss, Jeremy went from three to seven inches in twenty seconds.

Gabriel drove the Porsche to his place, which was in the new Hoboken twin towers known as River View Quality Erections. He had the top floor penthouse suite, of course. To Jeremy, the rest of the night was like a dream. They were both pretty buzzed, but young, so there was no retiring of hard-ons. They went at it all night long. Jeremy learned one thing that night, that would be set in stone for the rest of their relationship. He would always be pitcher and Gabriel would always be the catcher.

A pretty young blonde nurse would occasionally pop in the room to check on his condition. She was very sweet and would hold Gabriel's hand and rub his shoulders lightly. She confided to Jeremy that she was a huge fan and she was sure the angels were with him.

When she left the room, Jeremy looked down upon his hero and waxed nostalgic once again. He remembered another night, the night he layered on the vanilla cologne that was so highly recommended to him by a friend. Gabriel's reaction to it was immediate. He said, 'what the hell is that smell? Is that vanilla I smell? I hate that smell; it makes me hurl. Please, take a shower or something, the smell of vanilla truly gags me.' But that was Gabe, ever unpredictable.

Intensive care rooms are places where time melds with molasses. Hours went by, Gabriel hardly stirred. Jeremy prayed. 'Please, dear, Jesus, shine your light on my Gabe and get him through this.'

And so it was, Jesus must have waved his hand in their direction, for Gabriel survived the first night and eventually gained his strength back. He was released from the hospital two weeks later.

After three weeks at home, he was more or less back to himself, albeit not so interested in any kind of sex. Jeremy, ever the one to please, had, on more than one occasion, offered to gently jerk him off for medicinal purposes, only to be rebuffed by Gabriel with words like. "For Christ's sake, I just had a fucking transplant. Give me a break, would ya?"

During his convalescence, Gabriel developed an obsession to find out who his donor was. Ordinarily, that is not an easy thing to do. But because of his fame and his connections, he was able to eventually find the surviving family of his donor.

They lived somewhat close by, in the small hamlet of Happyfield, NJ. He decided to pay them a visit rather than just call.

The donor's parents lived on Washington Street, wide and tree lined, in one of the better sections of town. Gabriel knocked at the wide paneled walnut door. He guessed the man who answered the door was the father of the donor. He introduced himself and added at the end. "I am the recipient of your daughter's liver." To which the balding elderly gentleman replied. "You are mistaken; we have not had a daughter, alive or dead, for some time." He then slammed the door in Gabriel's face.

Gabriel went back and re-booted. He hired a private detective who in less than a week, was able to track down the donor's lover. Her name was Mary, Mary McCunlap.

With address in hand, he paid her a visit. She too, lived in Happyfield N.J. but not in the same neighborhood where he last visited. This address was obviously on the Catholic side of town. It was a twin home actually. He knocked.

He was not prepared for his own reaction when the door opened. There before him, was a twenty-ish, blue eyed, freckle faced, strawberry blonde; about five-feet-five, with a body not unlike that of a supermodel. She opened the door and said, "Yes, can I help you?" The sound of her voice was delicious and sweet, like a chocolate strawberry. Gabriel, possibly the gayest man that has yet lived on this earth, was tongue tied in the presence of such female beauty. He stammered awkwardly as he announced. "Uh, uh, I am the don-ee. I, a, have her liver in my upper abdomen." Having said this, he immediately hated himself for being such a putz. Equally caught off guard, and in the same stammering fashion the beauty replied. "You, you, mean you have Dik's liver, living inside of you?"

"Did you say Dick's liver," Gabriel said, now recovered somewhat. I was told my donor was female."

"Oh, I'm so sorry; this is such an emotional moment for me. Let me explain about the name. The love of my life was given the beautiful Armenian name Dikranouhi, which in their language means peace. It was her maternal grandmother's name. Naturally, her American nickname became Dik."

"I see. I hope I have not overreached my bounds by seeking you out."

She looked at him with searching eyes and said, "Wait. Are you Gabriel O'Gayhee, the famous Broadway star? I read all about your transplant. It never dawned on me that you may have received Dik's liver. Please, come in. I am so honored."

He followed behind her, and soon found he was hardly able to look at anything other than her, so very perfect, derriere. He had to force himself to glance about the room. She led him through a small living room, the walls of which were covered from mid height to ceiling with pictures of her and a stocky person with a crew cut, whom Gabriel assumed was her lover and his donor, Dik.

They passed through a small dining room and entered an even smaller kitchen. There, she pulled a stool for him and he sat down at a tiny table-lette that was fastened to the wall. She offered him an assortment of things to drink. He opted for sweetened ice tea. She had the unsweetened.

As she poured the tea for him she said, "Dik always drank the sweetened." She sat on the stool across from him and stared at him for a moment before she spoke. "You know, you're going to think I'm crazy and you look nothing like her, but the way you just took that first sip of your ice tea, you reminded me of my Dik. I see you're left handed?"

When she said this, Gabriel looked down at his left hand. It was cradling his glass. He never drank anything in his life with his left hand. The sight of which freaked him out a bit, and he immediately pushed the drink over to his right hand.

"So, are you right handed or left handed?" Mary asked.

"I'm a righty," Gabe answered.

They sat in that small kitchen drinking ice teas for the better part of two hours. Mary learned of Gabe's younger years and his theatrical climb up the ladder. He was careful not to elaborate about his sexual exploits, which were legendary anyway. For her part, she talked of her younger years as a Happyfield sports star and her participation in more than a few Happyfield High School state championships. She also, for some reason, told him of her first lesbian experience.

"I don't know why I'm telling you this, but it feels so natural to talk to you. My first week in ninth grade, here at Happyfield High, I was introduced to the new girl, Dikranouhi. I was old enough to see that she was butch, but I was strangely attracted to her. As it turns out, she was very aggressive. Near the end of my freshman year, at one of the endless parties that take place here in town when the parents are gone, she seduced me. I blamed the episode on drinking and did not so much as speak to her till the summer after college. I ran into her at a bar, and the rest, you might say, is history. We spent that night together and every night since then, until the accident that is."

Tears were now running down her freckled face. Gabriel was so moved by the emotion of the moment, that he got up from his stool, went over to her and held her tightly in his arms as they cried together for many minutes.

At one point, she looked up at him, wiped the tears from her cheeks and said, with a forced smile, "Sorry, I'm just not over it yet." Gabriel squeezed her close once again and said, as he wiped the tears from his own cheeks, "May I come by to visit with you again, or can we meet for a drink?"

"Sure! We should become BFF's." she said enthusiastically, now recovered a bit. "How about this Friday, at Alto's on Route 70, do you know of it?"

"No, but I'll find it, Shall we say seven-ish?"

"Perfect, I'll meet you at the bar."

With that, she walked him to the door. As he stood on the porch he said, "It's certainly true I never knew Dik, and these things, these transplants are so random, but somehow, strangely, I feel a connection with her and to you as well." He held her gaze for a moment, then turned and left.

When he got back home it was about eight p.m. Jeremy was watching TV in their spacious living room.

"So, did you meet the donor's relatives?" he said, a bit sarcastically, for he was only somewhat up-to-date on Gabriel's quest to find the donor's family. "I did," was all that Gabriel said.

"Well?" came the response.

"Well what?"

"Is that how it's going to be? You know you have been practically non-communicative with me ever since you have been on this trek to find out all you can about your donor. Are you shutting me out? Is that it?"

"Pay attention Jeremy," Gabriel said, in an elevated voice, "I will tell you what I goddamn please."

Jeremy responded with something, but Gabriel tuned him out as he walked down the hall slamming the door to the spare bedroom.

Jeremy was getting very frustrated. On the one hand, he tried hard to be sympathetic due to the trauma that Gabe had gone through, but on the other hand, some months had now gone by and things were just not the same between them.

Later, when Jeremy realized that he could not concentrate on the movie he was watching, he decided to retire. The genuine sweetness in him required that he knock gently on the spare bedroom door and ask Gabriel if he needed anything. Even though the light was still on, there was no response.

Gabriel heard the request. He was not sleeping, reading, texting, tweeting or watching TV. He was thinking. More accurately, he was obsessing, obsessing about Mary. He could not get the image of her out of his mind. The freckles, the tears on her cheeks, her ass, never in his life had he been so not in control. He was certain that he was losing his mind. He turned out the light and went to bed.

He could not sleep. After about an hour of flipping side to side, he decided to masturbate, for that had always been a sleep-inducing experience for him in the past. As he fiddled with himself trying to get hard he fanaticized about encounters he had had with Jeremy. Nothing was happening. He tried reliving bathhouse experiences, nothing, gay parking areas, nothing, seedy toilet stalls with anonymous penises pushed through makeshift holes, nothing, fiddling, fiddling, nothing, nothing. He eventually gave up and decided he needed to see his shrink.

The next day he did exactly that. Due to a cancelation, he was able to get a one o'clock appointment with Dr. Peter Von Schtupinchild. Dr. Pete, as he called him, knew him well. He was also gay, so it made these appointments more lighthearted and natural.

"So, Gabriel, I haven't seen you in what, nine months, is it? Did you fuck the entire cast this time or are you slowing down?" That little statement was exactly the reason Gabriel loved Dr. Pete. He knew his history so well and would often make quips like that to loosen Gabriel up in the event he had a real problem. And a real problem for maybe for the first time in his life, was exactly why he was sitting across from him now.

"Are you comfy? Relax and give it to me." That's what he always said. And Gabe gave it to him.

"I'm scared shitless, I think I have lost my gayness." Gabriel expected some outburst from the Schtuper but all he got in return was:

"Go on."

"Well as you know I was the queen of the galaxy before I met Jeremy. I mean you know by the sessions we've had that I would suck the cock of a death, dumb and blind man in a coma if he could get it up. In the dictionary under gay, male whore is a picture of me with no further description necessary."

"Your point being?"

"God damn you. What kind of a sadist are you? I need help here and you make a joke."

"Okay, calm down. Let's work this backwards. We know you had a serious surgery, right? So, in weeks or months, how long has it been since you had an orgasm, either alone, with Jeremy or others, for that matter?"

"Probably nine months."

"Well?"

"Well what, motherfucker? Why am I sitting here all fucked up, and I have to hear you say, *well?* Maybe you should pay me for the session as it seems I'm the one doing all the work."

"For one thing," the Schtuper said, "I've never fucked a mother, so just calm down a moment and let me think. I read or heard something recently... oh yeah, about a month ago, it was, I read an article about transplants that said something like, recipients of organs sometime experience strange and unnatural cravings that they did not have before the transplant. 'The article went on to say that when the recipient was able to find out information about the donor, that more often than not, the cravings were somehow transferred from the donor to the recipient. This bit of weirdness is very prevalent amongst organ recipients, and the experts are hard pressed to explain it. But you Gabe baby, you can google it. So, that's it. That's your homework. Follow the Google Brick Road and the wizard at the end of it will tell you all. Do this, my friend, and I will see you in two weeks."

Gabriel followed his doctor's instructions. To his amazement there were hundreds of individual stories of strange déjà vu like experiences, cravings, dreams, nightmares, you name it. So many organ recipients had these experiences that Gabriel could come to but one conclusion. Since he received a liver from a lesbian, he was now, somehow, leaning that way.

The next few days he sequestered himself in the spare bedroom, completely ignoring Jeremy. At one point, he made a decision. He came out of the room and confronted Jeremy. He said with little or no emotion. "Jeremy, you have to move out. Try to be out by Friday. I will be staying at a hotel till then, so as not to get in your way." For some reason, Gabriel thought that his statement would be obeyed and that would be that. He was wrong.

"Please don't do this to us," Jeremy pleaded now with tears in his eyes. "We love each other, I know this. You're just going through some sort of breakdown. Maybe you should go talk to Pete."

"I have seen Pete. I'm not having a breakdown. I'm a lesbian. There, now you know. I don't wish to hurt you, but I can't be with you anymore. Just move out and get on with your life." With that, he turned to retire to his room. He was not prepared for what happened next. Jeremy ran past him and tried to block the door to the spare bedroom, crying hysterically.

"You're not a lesbian. You're the gayest of the gay. You need drugs or something, that's all."

Gabriel decided it was time to leave. He turned to go, but Jeremy fell to the floor and latched on to one of his legs, sobbing over and over, "don't leave me. Don't, leave me." Gabriel dragged him toward the front door. When he got there, he pushed Jeremy off his leg and said, "Just be out by Friday. I put an extra ten thousand in your bank account." He closed the door behind him. He could hear the wailing all the way down the hall.

So, Jeremy moved out. When Gabriel returned to his condo on Friday afternoon, all that was left of Jeremy was a one-page hand written note. It read:

My dearest Gabriel,
  Know this. I love you with all my heart, body and soul. I will always love you. I know you will get over this lesbian nonsense, and you will come back to me. I will wait for you forever.
Love always,
Jeremy

Gabriel crumpled it up and threw it in the trash can. He had to get ready. He had a date with Mary.

He arrived a few minutes late. Mary was already there sitting at the bar of a posh restaurant. She was wearing a low cut white cotton summer dress with little aqua triangles printed on it. As before, she was stunning to look at. Gabriel hugged her hello and found himself looking straight down at her cleavage as he pulled away, and just for a split second, he spied the slightest hint of pink areole peeping out from her bra. As distracted as he was, he remained cool as they exchanged niceties. The bartender came up to them almost immediately. Mary ordered a Cosmo and Gabriel blurted out, "I'll have a Buttery Nipple."

"Coming right up," the bar-keep said.

"I have no idea why I just ordered that. I always drink a mint julep. It just popped out of my mouth. I don't even know what's in it."

"Oh, come on, it's such a complicated drink, you must have had it before. Coincidently, that particular drink was one of Dik's favorites. She would always order it on special occasions."

The drinks came and Gabriel again stated that he had no idea what was in it. Mary explained, its equal parts vodka, Irish cream, butterscotch snaps, and coffee liqueur. You'll love it." Gabriel was mighty leery about the Irish cream part, as he loathed vanilla. Nevertheless, he took a sip and was quite relieved that he liked it. As the night went on he had three more and was quite drunk. Mary insisted that he should not drive back home in his condition. She told him that he should return with her to her place, and that she would drive him back to get his car in the morning.

As they were walking up the steps of her porch Gabriel somehow twisted his ankle and almost fell down. Mary put her arm around him and helped him get through the door. He was quite wobbly, and at one point she was holding him up with both her arms around him. He then swung her around and he fell forward pinning her against the wall. Her lovely face was just inches from his. He decided he had to kiss her. She was having none of it. She turned her head away immediately and said, "You are drunk. You're getting obnoxious and you're going to sleep it off. With that she pushed him down on the couch where he conked out almost immediately.

The next morning, Gabriel awoke with a wicked headache. He could smell fresh coffee. He forced himself up and saw that Mary was sitting at the little kitchen table reading something. "Well good morning," she said as he plopped himself on the stool across from her. I'll get you a coffee and some ibuprofens." She handed him a glass of orange juice and said, "Here take these." He did as he was told and just sat there for a moment trying hard to remember anything from the night before.

"I feel like shit. Did I do anything stupid?"

"Not stupid really, maybe just a little inappropriate, you tried to kiss me. We both know that I am a lesbian and you are a gay man. So, what was that all about?"

"Well, I don't really know. I hardly remember anything, but you're wrong about me being a gay man." He was trying to sound rational but it wasn't working. "What I'm trying to say is -- I'm a lesbian."

"If you're a lesbian, then I'm Liberace," she said with a laugh.

"No really, It's, it's Dik's liver. I have become a lesbian because of Dik's liver. I can explain, actually." He took his iPhone from his pocket and googled, 'transplant recipients take on thoughts and habits from donors. He handed the phone to Mary, and she read a few of the case histories.

"You're trying to tell me that receiving Dik's liver, has turned you into a lesbian?"

"Bingo! And what's more, I'm certain that I'm in love with you." She pursed her lips together, squinted her eyes almost shut, recovered and said, Okay, let's go. I'm taking you to your car." He certainly did not like the sharpness of her response, but he was a master manipulator and knew just how to answer her. He got all smooth like.

"That's a good idea because I have to take my anti-rejection medication. Maybe we can go have some breakfast." She looked at him incredulously, for she was not going to fall for the con. "I'm taking you to your car. You can go have breakfast if you want, but I'm afraid this friendship is not working out. You have a screw loose or something. You better get some help. You obviously have some weird thoughts going through your head. I'll give you that. It may be somehow connected to your transplant, and that's all fine and dandy for you, but you must know one thing about me. I am a lesbian. I don't think I'm a lesbian, or wish I was a lesbian; I am one hundred percent lesbian. I cannot be with a man, and I mean gay or otherwise and you, my friend, are definitely a man."

"No, no, I'm a lesbian; really, I'm stuck in a man's body. You must believe me. I'm a transgendered individual." The more he talked the nuttier he sounded, even to himself.

She did not comment on his pleading, she simply said, "Let's go."

During the short ride to his car, he tried desperately to get his hung-over brain to work. After exploring about a million possible things to say he came up with this: "The next time you see me, I will be perfect."

She pulled into the parking lot and slid into the spot next to his Porsche and said, "Nice to have met you. Please don't come back."

The ride home for Gabriel was not as hard as one might expect, for he knew exactly what he must do. He would have a sex change.

And so, he did. He contacted the famous Italian sex reassignment surgeon, Dr. Absualuta Mutationato. After the initial consultation, the good doctor sent him off to see two very prominent transgender shrinks. One of which was the world-famous Dr. Phil McCracken. The other was a very thoughtful and helpful, transgendered individual, Dr. Munchma Quchi. The results were unanimous. Gabriel was a woman trapped in a man's body. The fact that he felt he was actually a lesbian trapped in a man's body didn't seem to matter much.

With the reports, back, Gabriel was free to receive reassignment therapy, such as hormone treatment and hair removal. When he had completed the protocol, he signed off for the surgery, which included small A-cup breast implants.

On November 4, 2015 Gabriel, for all intents and purposes, was now a woman, but more importantly to him, a lesbian.

Over the next few months, she had to learn certain things all over again. Everything was different. Peeing for instance, he, now a she, kind of missed standing up, and she thought that now that she was butch, she might try to perfect a standing up way to do it. She had no luck with that. The only way that worked for her was if she was standing naked in the shower. Walking was another thing. When she was a gay man, she had nice prancy kind of gait. But a butch would not walk that way. She had to change it. She tried a bunch of perambulations, and finally settled for a light stomping motion with a quick pace. She worked at it every day until it became natural to her. It took a total of six months to perfect her persona. As for her hair, she went to a flat top. She even gained about twenty pounds to perfect the look. She looked so different now, she could go almost anywhere and not be recognized. For all intents and purposes, she looked like your everyday, run- of-the-mill, butch. It was time to reintroduce herself to the fair femme Mary.

Mary worked as a paralegal for the law firm of Dix, Cox, and Kuntz. They specialized in sexual harassment lawsuits. Gabby, her new name, parked in front of their offices just around closing time. As Mary walked out of the building, Gabby, wearing baggy jeans and a red flannel shirt, got out of her car and came right up to her. Mary was as hot as ever wearing a navy business suit with a short tight skirt and four inch spikes. Gabby said, "Hello Mary." Mary stopped and stared for a moment and said, "Oh my god, it's you, isn't it?"

"I was hoping you would recognize me. Can I interest you in drink somewhere? I have so much to tell you."

"Well, I have an appointment at seven, but I guess I might have time for one," she said, too curious to say otherwise.

"We're pretty close to Alto's. Shall we go there," Gabby said?

"Alto's it is. See you there."

Gabby watched Mary for a moment as she walked to her car. She was lusting for her so bad at that moment, but she had to remind herself that this time around she shouldn't be so pushy, or take anything for granted. She would behave, as a perfect gentleperson, so to speak.

During the next half hour, Mary learned of Gabby's journey and how she felt so much more natural now that she was truly a lesbian. Mary admitted to feeling bad about how poorly she treated him/her when last, they met. Gabby reminded her that he was now a, *she*. She could, however, make it up to her, by having dinner with her, and that she now preferred to be called Gabby. They agreed that instead of going out, Mary would have her over to her place for dinner.

"Okay, Gabby, Saturday night at my place". Gabby walked her to her car and gave her a nice little hug and a cheek kiss.

That light interaction with her, right at the end, was enough to give Gabby that little electric shock she was frequently experiencing in the generously large clitoris they had fashioned for her. It was a curious feeling but not unpleasant.

Saturday night came and went quite well. This date was followed by a few more. On the third date Mary invited her in for a nightcap. The nightcap turned into two bottles of wine and soon they were both really buzzed. At one point, after a really long kiss on the couch, Mary said, "We're probably going to do this, aren't we?"

"I truly hope so" Gabby said. "But I want you to know I have zero experience with this kind of sex."

"Just relax, I'm a good teacher." With that, she led her up the narrow stairway to her room. She left the light on for a second while she lit two candles that were sitting on a mahogany nightstand. The room was certainly girly girl, with pink walls, white sheer window treatments, and white lace embroidered bedcovers. There were at least twenty pillows lying about. These she removed and stacked on a long mahogany side table.

"Come here Gabby, she said, let me undress you." Gabby was in a panic, but did as she was told. Mary removed her light-blue button-down shirt that had the sleeves rolled up to the elbow. Next, she removed her tight necked T-shirt.

When she had done this, she took the time to caress Gabby's perky little breasts, remarking as she did so, "These are so darling;

I think I could get used to these." Then she unbuckled Gabby's belt, undid the button, pulled her zipper down and let the khaki trousers fall to the floor. Gabby sat down on the edge of the bed as Mary removed the oxblood wingtips, black knee socks and the pants. Gabby was left wearing nothing but men's full sized briefs. Mary reached behind these, and as Gabby scrunched up. She pulled them off. She told her to spread her legs and lay back. This Gabby did, all the while in mortal terror of what might happen next. Nothing happened for a moment that is, for Mary took the time to fully inspect the results of the surgery, and then she remarked. "It's quite lovely really. They did a great job, and you have the biggest clit I have ever seen.

With that she lowered her mouth to it, and gave it a nice long suck.

Gabby was trembling now. It was partly the terror, but mostly because of the explosion of sensation she was feeling under Mary's expert machinations. She reached up with one hand and gently caressed, tweaked and pinched Gabby's hard little nipples.

Gabby had not been able to achieve an orgasm on her own; she was disappointed, and had brought this matter up with the surgeon. She was told that these things take time and patience, and that most get the hang of it eventually.

Soon, Mary was working her magic with her tongue. Slowly at first, and then going imperceptibly faster, her tongue flicking up and down, side to side, she added a clever little twirling motion. She was in no hurry. Soon, Gabby's hips were moving in rhythm with her tempo, faster and faster, as firmer pressure was applied. Now, Gabby was flipping about the bed like a beached brook trout.

And then it happened, the final movement of her hips practically knocking them both off the bed. Gabby's head exploded with pleasure. She felt for a second there that she might pass out. As she lay there slowly coming down from her first orgasm as a woman.

Mary got up from the bed, unbuttoned her blouse and removed it. Next went the skirt. Her perfect oversized breasts strained against the sized too small, bra. She reached back with her left hand, and popped the hook, while still holding her bra up with her right hand. She then gave Gabby a seductive wink and flung the bra across the room. Gabby literally gasped as she stared up at thirty-six, double D's, with silver-dollar sized areolas and Ticonderoga pencil-eraser nipples. Lastly, the pearl colored bikini briefs, were also flung across the room with another sexy wink. Her bush, as Gabby expected, was also strawberry blonde, but much thicker than she imagined.

She lay down next to Gabby, they kissed and caressed in the afterglow for a good long while. Mary spoke first, "Other than the size of that thing I would never think of you as anything but a woman. Do you know what comes next?

"No, what"

"Me, silly," She laughed. Gabby was beginning to get a bad feeling about something. Ever since Mary got naked, Gabby kept thinking she could smell vanilla. She desperately hoped it was her imagination. Nothing made her sicker than the smell of vanilla. She just came out with it. "Do you smell vanilla?"

"Uh, yes, of course."

Are you wearing that vanilla perfume?" Gabby asked, wondering how she was going to tell Mary to scrub the smell off her.

"No, not at all, vanilla is just my natural scent. Just say I'm lucky I guess. I'm sure you'll enjoy it. I've never met anyone who didn't. Now come on lover. I'm so excited.

Gabby was just about to tell her that she would soon be spewing cookies all over her bed, when she noticed something. She wasn't feeling nauseous after all. In fact, she was somehow enjoying the odor. She decided to go for it. Gabby kissed her hotly and proceeded with her part of the experiment.

Mary guided her through each step along the way. She fondled those magnificent breasts. She put her mouth on them, used her tongue on them, and soon had Mary breathing hard with her eyes closed. "That's it, you're doing great. Now go down on me."

She slowly kissed her way down across Mary's flat belly. When she got to the strawberry jungle, Mary spread and raised her legs. Gabby's head was now a few inches from what was, no doubt, the world's most perfect, plump, mons veneris. "Go for it Gabby, just like I did for you. I won't last long. I haven't had sex with anyone since my Dik passed.

With that she looked up at Mary, returned the same seductive wink, and tried her best to imitate everything Mary had done for her. Gabby was now surrounded by the taste and smell of vanilla, and loving it.

Sure enough, just a few minutes of this was all it took. Mary came violently, locking her long legs around Gabby's head, practically breaking her neck. She rhythmically rocked and squeezed Gabby's head like this for a long minute.

Finally, allowed to come up for air, Gabby looked up at a heavy breathing and very flushed Mary, and said, "How'd I do?"

"You did everything just perfect, but your face looks like a glazed donut. She grabbed a towel that was laying, neatly folded, at the foot of the bed. "Here use this."

This Gabby did, and they lay locked together for a long while exchanging sweet kisses and words of endearment. Mary suggested they take a shower together. After, they lay naked under the sheets, and fell asleep.

Gabby awoke first and with the morning light coming in through the eastern window, she had a chance to observe her prize in the daylight. The sheet they were sleeping under had fallen away. Mary was even more beautiful naked and without makeup than any women Gabby had ever seen, and she had seen a few, as women in the theater easily get naked in front gay men.

Mary was facing Gabby with her legs slightly apart. Her skin shade was the palest white. Her long, natural strawberry-blond, hair was cascading carelessly across those large D-cup breasts which were rising and falling with her gentle breathing. Her nipples seemed even pinker in the morning light. Her flat belly showed off a perky little belly button that was not quite an outie.

A vision of white and pink, that was Mary. And, of course, there was the smell of vanilla that wafted about the room. Gabby kissed her gently on the neck. Mary awoke, smiled at her and said, "I think I love you." They made love again.

Some months went by, and they were living together in Gabby's penthouse. They would soon have to move though, for there is not much work for a former gay musical star who was now unsalable. There was another problem, too. Gabby was beginning to get a little nauseous around Mary when her clothes were off. And then one night it happened. Gabby went down on Mary, only to come violently up, blowing chunks all over Mary's adorable belly button. That was pretty much it. Mary moved out the next day.

Gabby was sick to death over the whole mess. She spoke with the surgeon, the transgender shrinks. They were of no use. Finally, she decided to call her good friend Dr. Pete, whom she had abandoned and not seen for some months. She made an appointment.

"Holy Christ Almighty, I read about it, but I always thought it was a publicity stunt. What in the hell did you do?" is what the Schtuper said when Gabby walked into his office.

"At this moment, I'm not sure, but I know I need help," Gabby said with tears in her eyes.

"Start from the beginning."

The whole while that Gabby was relating the story, the Schtuper was staring at her in disbelief. When she finished, the doc said. "So, what do you want me to do? I can't fix this. This is way over my head. I deal mostly with sniveling little fairies like you were before, people who really don't have any problems. I'm sorry. It was really nice to see you again, but I can't help you."

Gabby went home and wept for two days. She was alone now, really alone, for possibly the first time in her life. Then she remembered the letter, the letter that Jeremy had left for her in the kitchen the day he left. 'What did it say, she thought to herself? Something like: 'I will always love you. I will always be here for you.' Of course, Jeremy did love her, and does love her. She decided to find him. She felt certain that Jeremy loved her for the person on the inside. He would take her back with open arms, even in this condition.

The more she thought about Jeremy, the better she felt. She ditched the dykey clothes, and put on a pair of flaming red slacks that she could not button at the waist. There was no camel cock to show off, and she thought for a moment about stuffing something in there. But then she thought there was no point in that because unless Jeremy lived under a rock, he would know all about the famous Gabriel becoming a lesbian. She threw on a sweater to hide the unbuttoned pants and sat down at the computer to try to locate the one true love of her life.

She got the address and headed right over. Surprisingly, it was quite close, and in a very expensive apartment building. She wondered how Jeremy could afford it.

She decided to walk over. On the way, she noticed a strange sky above. There were numerous white fluffy clouds flying quite low, like lower than the tops of the buildings even.

She entered the building, convinced the security guy of who she was and talked him into allowing her to head up unannounced.

As she ascended the elevator to the twenty-sixth floor she remembered exactly what Jeremy had written on that note.

Know this: I love you with all my heart, body and soul. I will always love you. I know you will get over this lesbian nonsense and you will come back to me. I will wait for you forever.

As the elevator doors opened she was so filled with love for Jeremy that she felt sure she would soon be in his loving embrace.

She rang the bell, and in just a few seconds she was looking into the eyes of an angel, but the angel didn't look all that happy to see her.

"What do you want and how did you get up here," the angel said, now with a few feathers falling off.

"Jeremy, I'm home, I mean I'm back, your letter, you said you'd always be here for me." Just then, there came a voice moving toward them from somewhere in the apartment.

"Honey, who are you talking to?" The voice said, as it arrived on the scene. A very large black man was now standing in front of her with his arm around Jeremy's shoulder. Gabby recognized him from the newspapers and media. It was Dixon Heiner, the star linebacker for the Jets and the very first NFL player ever to come out.

Gabby could hear the words in her head, the words that Dixon used at the press conference when asked if he thought he might receive some flak from his teammates about his open gayness. To this he answered: *To any and all of y'all, who think they might have a problem with this, keep in mind that the only thing I like better than suckin' cock, is kickin' ass.*

The big man looked down at the frightened lesbian and said, "Git," as he slammed the door in her face.

Gabby's mind just went blank; she ran down the hall to the elevator.

The next thing Gabby remembered was standing on the edge of the roof of her building, twenty-five stories up. She was calm now, and just standing there looking at the fluffy white clouds as they floated by. One, in particular, looked comfy and was just the right size, very inviting indeed, and she just a stepped off on to it.

The End

For alternative ending, read on,

One, in particular, looked so very comfy and was just the right size, very inviting indeed, and just a step away. Gabby stepped off onto it and found it to be not unlike a big marshmallow. She sat down on it and enjoyed the peaceful ride. She looked out and saw that she was not the only one occupying a cloud. There were others, all sitting like her on top of their clouds.

A sunset, from the point of view of a cloud, is quite remarkable. Brilliant pinks and blues, along with all the subtle colors of the rainbow rolled into one. Gabby was loving this sunset. All her recent troubles seemed to be melting away.

As the sun kissed the tiniest point on the horizon, a laser-like shaft of brilliant white light shot from that spot strait up to infinity, then disappeared. Everything was now black, black beyond black.

Gabby eased slowly back onto her cloud. She felt only love, self-love. She fell fast asleep.

The warmth of the morning sun was her alarm clock. She sat up and looked about. Below her were thousands of tiny islands surrounded by beautiful aqua marine water. Each island had a few palm trees and a beach chair. Sitting alone on each beach chair, were the most beautiful and perfect people Gabby had ever seen, alone, totally alone, each and every one. Her cloud was moving slower now and lower. It came to a stop on an empty island. Gabby stepped off. When she did so, she was no longer Gabby. He was the beautiful Gabriel once again. He walked over to his beach chair and sat down.

There will always be a mint julep. There will always be a sunny day. There will always be a Gabriel, and he will always be alone.

This is enough

WOODEN SCREENS

I remember the day Maggie, my Boston Terrier, brought her to me. It was early June, a warm, sunny, South Jersey morning. I was sitting at my kitchen table intently reading the sports section when the bell rang, with two close together insistent rings. Ding dung, ding dung. My bell had this flat second note. I was always telling myself I should replace it, but I never really got around to it. I said out loud to no one, "Who in the hell could this be?" I flip flopped through the house to the front door, and opened it without peeking through the blinds.

There, standing on my front porch, with Maggie in her arms, was a vision of loveliness if ever there was one. Her slightly wide set dark eyes, were fixed on me with a stony squint. Her right eye squinched down a bit more than the left. With an icy tone, she said, "Is this your dog?"

"Why…a… yes," I stammered, "she must have jumped the fence or something, I …. a… don't know?"

So completely blown away by the sight of such beauty on my porch, I could do little more than babble like an idiot. Her stare, still anchored, but now with both eyes in full squint, further reduced me to some kind of a liquid state. In a slightly higher, but nonetheless, General Patton's voice, she said, "Some people should pay a little more attention to their pets." She shifted Maggie to her right hip, the way a mother might balance a toddler. Curiously, her eyes were now quite wide.

She stood there unblinking for what seemed to me like a full week. Ten seconds, but as dumb struck, and squirmy as I was, it seemed that long to me.

I wondered what happened to my usual unwavering salesmanship ability. The suave coolness under pressure that I always seem to be able to call on at will. Alas, these traits were on lock-down at the moment.

I looked down to gaze at Maggie, who was staring back at me with those bugged out lizard-like, Boston eyes. She looked the way a calf might look, just before it became veal.

I slowly and sheepishly looked up at the holder of my dog. As dumbstruck as I was, my eyesight, nonetheless, was as keen as ever. I took the second half of the week to peruse the startling, implacable image that was set there before me. Dressed conservatively, in a grey knee length skirt with one of those form fitting ribbed white blouses. The top two buttons undone, revealing what seemed to be breasts that were bit too large for her thin frame. All this, floating under a long, Audrey Hepernesque neck.

She appeared to be in her early to mid-twenties, with long, black, silken hair. Fairly tall, I guessed about 5'-8".

Her eyes, were the pancakes though, dark brown, with extra-large pupils. The inky blackness of them spilled out and covered me like syrup.

Dark stars, with long thick, lashes, floating just below a natural and faultless, brow.

As I finished this survey, she gently placed Maggie down. The chunky, short haired gecko looked up at me for a second, with an *Oh shit, I did bad* look, and then scampered off.

The loveliness blinked, "You're lucky I was walking by outside, or she may have been run over," she said in a voice, now strangely civilian like. Her eyes softened for a split second as she turned and walked away. I wanted to say something, but I couldn't draw the cowardly salesman out of his hiding place.

I flip flopped a few steps to the edge of my porch and leaned against the top rail, the better to gaze at her as she walked up the street. The vision of her got smaller in perspective as she walked the five hundred or so, feet to the corner. Her legs were long with gorgeous calves that tapered off perfectly at her ankles. From the front or the rear, she was a goddess.

I continued to watch as she turned the corner onto Colonial Street.

I lingered there on my porch. Replaying the scene as it had played out just moments before. Only one thought came to my mind, I was smitten. Of that there was no doubt. When I came back to earth, I said to myself out loud. "Whoever she is, she must think I am such a jerk."

I went back inside and spotted Maggie, still with the guilty look on her face; I let myself temporarily off the hook. "Maggie! How could you do this to me, make me look so irresponsible?"

Fall became winter. On a few occasions, I would get a glimpse her up on The Queens Highway our Main Street here in Happyfield, the little hamlet in which I lived.

A hard-snowy winter abruptly turned to spring.

I was a bit of a distance runner. I ran a few miles, about three times a week. During the spring, summer and fall, I ran as many five K's as I could fit in with my schedule. The first race of the year was held at the Cooper River. The race was a 4-mile loop. Typical, in that it had the usual macadam track that meandered around the ins and outs of the shape of the river. Some very nice shade trees were scattered here and there between large areas of nicely manicured turf.

On that day, at twenty-six, I was running in the 25 to 30 age category. Clad in my slightly worn "Aesic Gels", way too short and silly, Nike running shorts, and my "South Jersey Athletic Club" wife beater T-top.

I ran the race and finished 5th out of 35 in my age group. I was out of the money so to speak, but I liked these races. I was happy to be healthy and competing at a fairly high level; as the runners in this race were the crème de la crème of runners.

I really put on a kick at the end, barely beating out a fellow runner in my age group, just as we crossed the finish line. I was spent, hot and red faced, as only the Irish can look at the end of a race. I went right for the water jug. After gulping down about ten four ounce cups, I was just sort of looking around. That's when I laid eyes on her. There she was talking to my friend, Ben. I made a bee line to the very spot they were standing.

"Ben, buddy," I said, as I approached them. The sweat was pouring off me. I usually ran with a hat which I was now holding in my left hand. I tried to brush my hair back with my right hand as I approached them. I was sure I had hat head, and probably looked a fright.

Ben was his usually frumpy self. He had long since cornered the market for dressing poorly. Today he was sporting a way too tight, for a guy with a gut, red and white, horizontally striped t-shirt and green plaid mid-thigh length shorts. "Hey Ben, how have you been? I noticed you didn't race today. What's up with that? Is it that hammy again?" I said, referring to his many hamstring pulls. As I talked to his disheveled self, I was trying with all my might, not to stare at the apparition standing next to him. "So, who might this be?" I said to Ben, as I slowly and deftly turned my gaze towards the angel.

"This is Donatienne," he said.

"Donatienne, what an unusual name." I said, immediately whishing I had not said, unusual. "I think I know you, I mean we've met, but not formally, I think. Right?" I knew my pie-hole was open, but I seemed to have no control over the gibberish that was spewing out of it. Pleased to meet you," I said, trying to fix a blanched look on my face. She looked back at me, with an equally blanched, but not contrived blanched look. "Yes, you're the dog owner, I remember you." then she looked down at the dirt saying nothing more. I so, got the impression that she wanted nothing to do with me, that after a few more insincere niceties with Ben, I slinked away saying "Catch you later, Ben. Nice meetin ya, Donatienne." (I could only hope I repeated her name correctly, for I had never heard such a name before).

It really bugged me though, that she so easily ignored me. I am not a bad looking guy. I was in great shape. What was up with this Donata-whatever, that she would dis me so? Did she like Ben? Were they an item? Ben was tall, about six-five, and more than little overweight. He was fairly famous, though, having won a Grammy as a song writer. As far as I was concerned, that explained it. She was attracted to him because he was famous.

As it happened, we were in the local Starbucks a few weeks later. We, that being the local Sunday morning runners and I, had just finished a ten miler. The usual running stories were being told. When I had a chance to talk I queried as to who, if anyone, knew who That pretty brunette was I had seen with Ben at that particular race. One of my running buddies, Jim, filled me in. "You must mean Donatienne," he said.

"Yeah, that's her name," I said, now remembering the pronunciation. "What's their story?"

"They used to be an item. In fact, they lived together for a while but I guess it didn't work out, cause she moved out about six months ago. They're still friends though. Why are you interested in her?"

"Nah," I lied, "Just curious."

Out of this whole crowd I liked Jim the best. He was so open and easy to talk to. A lot of runners are sort of solitary types but not Jim; he had a special warmth that the others seemed to lack. I really didn't know a whole lot about him, but I did know he was a good family man.

The first time I met him was at a barbecue. He was there with his wife and two kids. I took note of how openly affectionate he was with her and how he doted on those little kids. He seemed to have the whole thing going, if you know what I mean. Someone told me once that he was a widower before he met his current wife, and had quite a different life than the one he has now.

It's now about eight months later. It's a Monday, about noon, on an unseasonably warm day for December. I'm exiting the running store where I just purchased a new pair of Gels. I started up Queens Highway. Not a highway really, but more or less a Main Street, with wide sidewalks, lined with high end shops. This is the little historic colonial hamlet known as The Borough of Happyfield, and the town where I live. I also get a large percentage of my work from the good folks who live here.

I was certainly down in the dumps lately, wondering why I didn't seem to have much luck finding a for real, for real, girlfriend. Most of my buddies were married by now. Some even had kids. I often wondered what kind of husband and dad I would be. I felt I was pretty well adjusted to life. I mean especially under my particular set of circumstances. I did have a couple of promising dates lately, but as usual, I found something about them I didn't like. I decided to change the subject on myself. I pushed my thoughts to last Sunday's Eagles' game and how I was sure the coach was an imbecile, when, suddenly, I was wrenched into the here and now by the sight of her. She was walking towards me on Queens's Highway.

I made up my mind right then and there to make her acquaintance properly, and maybe set a little ground work to meet with her for a coffee or something. Hoping I have her name right, I say in a loud voice, "Donatienne." She looks at me for a moment, then corrects me. "Dah-NAT-ienne, the emphasis in on the second consonant, not the first."

"Dah-NAT-ienne," I repeated (now proud of myself for getting it right). "Donatienne is that a Russian name," I said? She crinkled her eyes, as if she were incredulous at the question and said, "No, French." She then said, with a slight glare, "I hope you're keeping a better eye on your dog. A small dog like that could easily get run over you know." Before I could say anything in my defense, she resorted to a monotonous robot's voice and said, "Nice to see you again, in a hurry, late for work." She turned and walked away. I was only able to feebly say. "A… see ya."

As I too, walked away, I wondered to myself; she did say, nice to see you that's something. I looked back at her every few seconds to see where she was going, hoping that she wouldn't catch me. I watched as she walked into a store on the corner of Queens Highway and Carpenter Street. I took note of which store it was.

As I walked the four blocks to my house. I wondered, maybe she works there?

As luck would have it, I ran into Ben the very next morning at Starbucks.

"Ben, buddy," I said to him in a jovial way. "How have you been? I haven't seen you since the river run. You were with that gorgeous creature."

"Oh, you mean Donatienne" he said. "She and I lived together for a short time. It didn't work out but we remain good friends. I know what you're getting at. Forget it, she's not your type." *What did he mean by that?*

"I'm not interested in her, I was just remarking how pretty she is. I guess you didn't know, but I'm practically spoken for." I lied.

I decided to give him a shot back. "She must not be your type either."

"Okay smart ass. She and I broke up, sure, but it was mutual." He lied.

"So," I said, "What's her story?" I regretted giving him that little jab because I could sense that he was now annoyed with me and he probably wouldn't give me the kind of information that I really wanted. He went into some kind of "Zen" bullshit answer as only Ben could.

"What can one say about Donatienne? She is a saint, a devil, brilliant, naïve, sexy, cold and a hundred other oxymorons all rolled into one, a girl of such complexity that mere mortals, such as you and I, could never hope to truly understand her. Furthermore--- (*yeah, yeah, I thought* to myself, *what a fucking whack you are.* I knew I had to get him off this Freudian rant quickly, or I would have to listen to his insane ass for the next hour or two. I interrupted him in mid-sentence, saying, "Just answer me this, does she work at that little crystal ware shop up the street on the corner?" That stopped him dead in his tracks and with a bit of a glare he said, "Yes, she does, but like I said, she's not your type." I shot a quick look at my wrist, where a watch should have been. "Oh shit, gotta go, I'm late," I said, I fist bumped with him, and out the door I went. So, now I was sure of where she worked. I was starting to feel like a stalker.

As I said, I'm not a bad looking guy, six feet; broad shouldered, an athletic body, not so much because I work out but mostly from my work as a self-employed carpenter or Home Improvement

Specialist to be more precise. After graduating from Rutgers with a marketing degree, I decided to continue in the family tradition, in the trades, so to speak, my dad, my uncles, my cousins, all of them, were, or are, tradesman of one kind or another. I was the first one in my family to get a degree, and here I was working for a living. But I didn't mind at all. My grandfather and my granny, on my dad's side, raised me and my two sisters. Our parents were killed in a freak accident. It's inevitable that sooner or later after I meet someone who does not know the story will ask "What happened to your parents, how did they die, how did they pass? My answer always seems so unbelievable. It either stops them dead in their tracks or it stirs their interest to want to know more, the gory details if you will. I usually just come right out with it. "They were killed in the train wreck of 93. Did you ever hear of it?" Most people my age or older know of it. Seventy-four people died that day. Historically, the worst train wreck in New Jersey.

I really don't remember them. Pop, my grandfather, would talk of them often. My sisters, both older than me, would also never miss a chance to tell me about them. I guess they felt worse for me because I was so young when it happened. I, on the other hand, felt worse for them because they remembered them. Apparently, it was my mom and dad's greatest wish that their only son, go to college. My pop would remind me of their wish almost daily, as I was growing up.

"College is a good thing, boy. It'll round off the rough edges," he used to say. Sadly, he never got to see me graduate. A stroke took him about three months before I got my degree. He didn't suffer though. He was unconscious from the start of it and he never came around. He lived a year and a month after granny passed. They were such a sweet old couple. I think it was because they had a lot in common. Especially that slightly irreverent sense of humor they both shared. I miss the way they would banter back and forth with wise cracks and stuff. He would say things like, "It looks like you're limping again old girl." She would come back at him with something like, "No I ain't. It must be that twitch in your eye actin up on you again, you old fart." I surely do miss those old buggers.

So anyway, this remodeling thing is what I do best, having worked at it almost every summer and most weekends since I was fourteen. I built my first addition on my own the summer before I went to college. I dug the footings, poured the concrete, lay in the block, framed it up, electric, insulation, drywall, siding, roofing, and trim, all of it. This is what a real remodeler does, soup to nuts.

Now I know a thing or two about marketing. Something the rest of my family didn't know much about. I'm sure I'm going to hit the big time. Now all I need is someone to share my future with.

The years I spent working and going to school didn't leave much time for a real love life. I dated a few girls, and got plenty of sexual experience at Rutgers, also affectionately nicknamed "Bangers U", There was one girl though, in my senior year. She was a year older and in the first year of her Masters. I fell head over heels for her. I fell in love with her in about a week. I let my feelings be known, maybe a little too soon. I think this sort of spooked her. Anyway, as it turned out, she didn't feel quite the same way. She let me down softly though, even shedding a tear or two with me on our last night together. I had a few sleepless nights over her, but all in all, I think I recouped fairly well. Getting over things is a strong trait of mine.

About a week later, I had occasion to be in Starbucks again. It was a nice day. As I exited, I decided to take a walk down the block. As I approached the shop where she supposedly worked, I glanced through the window and, sure enough, there she was, showing something or other to a customer. I took only the briefest of glances. She was looking away so she did not see me. I was greatly relieved that I had performed this little reconnaissance, incognito. After that I drove by that intersection as often as I could, even if it was slightly out of my way. I was now, one cent short of a stalker.

I had the occasion to talk to one of the runners, who was a close friend of Ben's. I casually asked him if he knew her and if he knew where she lived. He answered. "Oh, she's a nanny for a woman with two kids, who lives on Colonial Street. I'm pretty sure she lives there too." "Holy shit," I thought to myself, that's the street that dead ends into my street.

Now, I was a regular traveler on Colonial, but try as I did, even driving down that street as slow as I could, I never saw hide nor hair of her. Eventually, I gave up thinking about her altogether and started dating a nurse, named Chloe.

That relationship lasted about two months. I ended it for the same reason that I thought it was so promising in the first place: sex. On or about the third date, this little nursey did me like I'd never been done before. So, insane and intense was the sex that I thought I would never tire it, but I did, tire of it. No sooner would we finish one marathon session then she would want to start all over again. Sounds good on paper, but try it in real life. It will wear you out. So, one morning I took her for a short walk and more or less told her that I was not that into her. She didn't take the news too well, and called me and texted me for about a month trying to get me to change my mind. I would always answer her and try to explain. I guess she eventually took the hint.

A few months go by. My love life is non-existent. It's a warm Sunday morning about 10:00 am, on the ninth of June, I was coming back from eating breakfast at the local diner. I decided to turn down Colonial street which, by this time, had become my normal route. My car is in for repairs, so I'm driving my truck, the windows are down and the music is blaring from my favorite oldies channel. As I approach the end of Colonial. I notice that Gloria, a neighbor of mine who lives in a twin home on the corner of Colonial and Lake street, is waving her arms frantically for me to pull over. I stop and say, "Hey, What's up?" Gloria is a slightly overweight, matronly woman about fifty, nice as hell though, and the possessor of a killer funny personality. I often thought that but for a quarter century we may have been a good match. I always shoveled her sidewalk in the winter, as I did for about a half dozen other neighbors who were not quite up to it.

In an overly desperate tone of voice, Gloria said, "Thank God you happened along, and with your truck too. I'm on my way to a wedding and I'm afraid I've locked myself out. My keys are on the kitchen table. I'm pretty sure my bedroom window is open. Maybe you can put your ladder up to the porch roof and climb through the window and get my keys."

As I glanced at the twin home, I noticed that the For-Rent sign was gone and that maybe Gloria and I had a new neighbor. I said to her, "Sure Gloria no problem."

I took the ladder off my truck, placed it up against the porch roof and climbed up and tried the window. Now I could tell the main window was open but the screen on the storm window was locked. I told her as much, and I also told her I had a special tool to remove the screen without damaging it. I came back down the ladder. I was rummaging through my truck for the tool when, to my astonishment, Donatienne comes walking down the porch steps of the other half of Gloria's house and said, "What's going on Gloria?" Gloria explains to her the circumstances of her dilemma. I was sure that Donatienne didn't yet know that I was about to walk right by her with the tool I needed. She looked up, just as I walked by.

"Hi Donatienne," was all I said, as I walked by her and went back up the ladder. I could plainly hear Gloria's voice as I fiddled with the screen as she sort-of talked loud anyway.

"So, Donatienne, do you know our neighbor, Rick?"

"I ran across him once or twice," she answered.

"Well let me tell you something about him, he is the best neighbor anyone ever had. He shovels the snow for just about all of us. He mows the lawns. He does all sorts of little fix up things. He is exceptional. Ya just gotta love him. For instance, at this very moment he is removing my screen so he can climb through my bedroom window and fetch for me, my keys, that I so carelessly left on my kitchen table. I'm already late; but wouldn't ya know it, and as luck would have it? No, come to think of it, luck has nothing to do with it. It just seems that Rick is always there when you need him. I tell you it's uncanny or something."

I'm hearing all this and I whisper to myself. "Yes, at last, some good publicity." I carefully removed the screen. I got the keys off the kitchen table and walked out of Gloria's house triumphantly, keys held high, for all to see. Donatienne is now standing next to Gloria. Gloria thanks me and gives me a great big hug, and further glorifies my persona to Donatienne, by saying, "I'm telling you Donatienne, if you ever need some help, or a favor or something, this guy is always there for ya."

Gloria got in her car, blowing kisses at me as she drove off. I very coolly looked over at Donatienne and said. "She blows kisses to all the guys in the neighborhood."

"You seem to be special around here," Donatienne said, making eye contact with me for the first time since the dog incident. Also, she has just uttered seven words to me. At least four words more than I ever got out of her before.

"Just being neighborly," I said.

"May I borrow that ladder?"

"What for?"

"I need to wash these porch windows and I think I might put the wooden screens in. They have been in the basement for God knows, how long." She said.

She doesn't know it, but my head is spinning, we are actually having a conversation. I made up my mind to deposit myself in cool and aloof mode. I answered her in a friendly but plain tone. "This ladder will not do. It's too tall. What you need is a step ladder. About a six-footer, I would guess. I have one in my shed. I'll get it for you."

I put the big ladder back on my truck and drove the half block to my driveway, got the step ladder and carried it back to her house on foot. I set it up for her in front of one of her porch windows and said, "There ya go, all set."

"Thanks," she said. I turned and walked toward my house as cool as a cucumber, without looking back.

I poured myself an iced tea and went out on my front porch.

About a year ago, I installed this really cool porch swing, just big enough for two. I had a nice cushion made for it. It was kind of like an outdoor love seat. I sat down and brought myself to a slow easy glide.

I could see her plainly from this vantage point. I watched as she retrieved some old dusty screens from her basement. She pushed one of them up the step ladder and tried to put it in place. It wasn't fitting properly, and try as she did, it just wouldn't slip in. I watched in amusement as she returned with a hammer and proceeded to try to bash the thing into place. It was just about then, that I decided to walk across the street to her rescue.

"Donatienne," I called out as I approached her, "Would you allow me to help you out here?"

I continued in a knowledgeable tone of voice, "These old porches usually don't have proper footings. The freeze-thaw cycle over many winters tend to make them sink. That's why so many older porches seem to be leaning forward. If someone came along and installed openings for screens, they would almost assuredly have to be refitted every year or so. By the looks of these screens, they probably haven't been installed in many years.

"I'll need some tools to remedy this situation." I said

"Well, thanks a lot, but I don't really want you to go to any trouble for me."

"It'll be nothing, really." I returned with a set of saw horses, a circular saw, a tape measure, a carpenter's square, a pencil and a block plane. I climbed the ladder and used the square to determine how much I would have to cut off each screen. I was in my element. She said nothing, and just allowed me to work. Very few women wouldn't be impressed with the speed and accuracy in which I worked. After cutting each screen, I ran the plane over the raw cut edge to make it true and smooth for painting. Within about twenty minutes the screens were reshaped. I tried them out one at a time. They fit perfectly. The old screening however was dry and brittle with numerous holes. I told her that I might have some screening in my shed. I returned with what turned out to be just enough screening to finish the job.

I worked so quickly and efficiently that I impressed even myself. I was careful not to have any eye contact with her while I worked. I didn't want her to think I was showing off. The job being done, I turned to face her and she was beaming. The first real smile I had seen on that beautiful face was now directed at me. She said, "Thank you, thank you so much. It was wonderful to watch you work. You are truly a master." I was feeling mighty good about myself at that moment. I smiled at her, gave her a wink and said. "It's what I do, is all." She thanked me yet again. I got my tools together and said. "Think nothing of it. It was my pleasure."

I turned and schlepped myself and my tools across the street to my house. It was now about noon. I left the house to run some errands, and do some food shopping, with a trip to the liquor store to re-supply my "Coors Light". I returned about four. I took a leisurely shower, spent some time on the computer and started to think about dinner.

Ding dung. The front door bell croaked. Maggie started to bark. I shushed her as I walked across the room and opened the door. There, standing before me, was Donatienne, but this time, instead of Maggie in her arms, she was holding two bottles of beer, "Yuengling", to be exact. "I don't know if you drink beer, but I had these two bottles of "Yueng" in my fridge, and I thought you might like to share them with me."

Now my Pop had a saying for a moment such as this. I confess here, that I never really knew what he meant by it till that moment. The saying went "I feel as if I've been gently stroked across the brow with a chrysanthemum petal."

Here she was, after all this time, standing at my doorstep, smiling up at me, with two bottles of beer in her hands, apparently wanting to get to know me.

"Great," I said, "we can sit on the swing." I certainly didn't tell her I was a Coors Light guy, and that I never drank anything else. I opened both bottles easily twisting off the tops with my bare hands, chaliced as they were, it was no problem. "A toast to new neighbors," I said, the bottles clinked. She looked straight into my eyes. And gave me a little wink. From my point of view, the chemistry was obvious. I took my first sip of the Yuengling, ever. I was surprised at what a smooth taste it had, somehow, I knew I would never drink Coors Light again.

On that perfect summer night, on that wonderful swing, me pushing it ever so gently back and forth, she revealed to me all the things I longed to know about her. An only child from a small Pennsylvania town near Scranton, her mother and father both died when she was young. Her mother died when she was just two, of ovarian cancer. Her father died five years later, from a brain aneurism. She was raised by her maternal grandmother who is now seventy-two, and living alone in the same house she was raised in. Jeese, we're both semi orphans I thought to myself.

She told me of her brief affair with my friend Ben. He was so manic that no relationship was possible. She talked of her Icelander guy. How it held so much hope for her but one day without warning he announced to her that the relationship was not working for him and he left without a trace. She was devastated of course. She gave it a few days and then decided to try to find him. After some inquiry with some mutual friends, she found out that he had a wife in Iceland and they had been corresponding and he opted to go back home and make a go of it. He just left her in a lurch. To her, it was life as usual. The people she loved or would have loved just vanished. A lost soul was she, which, as you might imagine, made her all the more alluring. to me.

It occurred to me that she had more in common with me than anyone I had met up to this point in my life. Whatever I might have been thinking when I first met her, I now felt something like an obligation to help her see, that it doesn't always have to be just bad outcomes. That something was heading her way that would take away all the pain and loneliness.

Somehow, I knew, that night, on my perfect little porch, I was meant to come into her life. We talked and laughed about her shyness. How, whenever I tried to talk to her, her head would be pointing down, looking at the sidewalk or anywhere except at me. She told me that her shyness was a manifestation of her inability to trust anything, let alone anyone. She stopped here for a moment. She curiously and seriously looked into my eyes as if she might find comfort in them. I said nothing. After a period of about twenty seconds she said, "You see, I can look into your eyes."

We rocked and talked on that swing for hours. It was getting dark. I kept a CD player on the porch. I asked her if she wanted to hear some music and what she might like to hear. She said, "Anything you like, I'm not particular." I was a little worried that she might not like my taste in music. I had been raised on oldies, mostly getting that trait from my Uncle Bruce who was sort of a surrogate older brother to me. It was uncle Bruce, who often drove me to school events and sporting events. He would always be playing and singing along with his oldies. I would often join in. I said to her "How about some tunes from the seventies."

"Okay, great" she said, "I love the oldies." I was relieved to hear that, as I owned just about nothing after 1990.

I put on a "Simon and Garfunkel" CD. We listened to a couple of their old classics and then I switched to the next CD, my favorite of all times,

"Boz Scaggs." She mentioned it was getting a little chilly so I boldly put my arm around her just as Boz started with his magic. We sat close, in silence. We listened to "Lido Shuffle" and a couple of others, Then the classic "Love, look what you've done to me." She moved even closer to me and put her head on my shoulder, just as the song began. This song became for me, that night, my favorite of all time.

"Hope they never end this song
This could take us all night long
I looked at the moon and I felt blue
Then I looked again and I saw you

Eyes like fire in the night.
Bridges burning with their light
Now I want to spend the whole night through
And honey yes I'd like to spend it all with you.

Chorus:
Love, look what you've done to me
Never thought I'd fall again so easily
Oh, love, you wouldn't lie to me
Leading me to feel this way……

They might fade and turn to stone
Let's get crazy all alone
Hold me closer than you'd ever dare
Close your eyes and I'll be there

After all you are the one
Take me up the stairs and through the door
Take me where we don't care anymore
Chorus,
Twice.

At the end of that song, we were looking in each other's eyes.

I leaned forward and kissed her. I kept my eyes open as our lips met. Her eyes were shut. I was sure the words and the emotion of that song had won her over. I pulled her even closer to me. I could feel her heartbeat against my chest. I closed my eyes for the second kiss. At the first touch of our lips, some special place in my mind, the spiritual part, took my soul for a flight, winging somewhere in supernal place, the lonely heart I hid so well, being rebuilt before my eyes, goosebumps covered my flesh. As we came off this magical kiss, my sense of time and space was certainly off, lost in a fog not wanting to be found. Our lips parted with an elastic slowness, as if they were in a conspiracy to stay joined a bit longer. I held her tightly against me, as my flesh eased back to smooth.

Again, I could feel her heart beating against my chest, but now, much stronger and faster, the rhythm of her sweet breath, fell across my neck like rose petals, I was smitten, and I dared hope she felt the same.

When the time was right, we unwrapped ourselves from that embrace. I spoke first. As much as I wanted to say something else, I instinctively knew I had to play it cool here and not tip my hand. "Well that was good. Maybe we can try it again tomorrow." There was a slight pause. I watched intently as she took a deep breath and exhaled,

"I haven't been kissed like that in some time. I'm looking forward to tomorrow," she said. With my brain, now all mushy, I answered her with the most matter of fact voice I could muster. "Tomorrow then."

We stood and walked to the top of the steps. I said to her just before we descended, "Do you like Italian? How about we have dinner tomorrow at the new Italian restaurant up on the Highway?"

"That would be very nice. I've wanted to try that place," she said. She turned to face me. And said, Thanks, thanks for everything." I wanted to say something else, but instead I said, "Shall we call it a night; I'll walk you over."

"Okay, yes, I am a little worn out." I held her hand as we walked across the street and up to her front door. I thought about what kind of good night kiss I'd give her. I opted for something short. I bit her lip ever so gently at the end of that kiss,

"Tomorrow then," I said. I turned and walked home, on cloud nine, with those crazy chrysanthemum petals, bouncing across my forehead.

I entered my house, shut the door and shouted out.

"YES!"

I pumped my fist into the air. Sleep did not come easily that night.

I never did ask her what time she normally got up. As for me, I'm an early riser, up at six every morning, no matter what day it is.

I usually head to Starbucks for a latte. This beautiful perfect morning was no different. I walked to Starbucks, had my latte and told lies of the bull with my friends as usual. We solved all the problems of the world in about a half hour, as we always do, then I headed back home.

My house needed a little sprucing up, as this was the odd week between the visits from the cleaning lady. I put on the Michael

Jackson CD "Thriller," and proceeded to dance and sing my way through the housekeeping. Maggie was having none of it, she ran up to the third-floor bedroom to hide under the bed. I was feeling so good, I sang along, "Wanna be Startin Somethin", as I scrubbed the toilets, tubs and sinks, wielding the toilet bowl brush like an espy, stabbing at the air, me, the cleanser, the Windex, paper towels, everything, spinning and dancing as if it were choreographed, just for this special morning. I saved the vacuuming for last, dancing with the machine to "Billie Jean", cranked up as loud as it would go. I finished just as the song ended, took a bow to no one, and headed for the shower.

There, naked, leaning against the shower wall, with icy cold-water cascading over my overheated body, I said, out loud to myself, "So what now? Will you screw this up, Ricky boy? This is no ordinary girl here. She is so very special and most probably so fragile that you will most likely blow this." I paused at that point, realizing just how long I had been talking to myself, and switched to regular thinking. *Be natural. I think she would know if you were not, be as cool as permafrost. Don't blow this Ricky boy. Don't fuck this up.* I stayed in that cold shower for about twenty minutes, until I felt I was cool enough, and suave enough to emerge.

We had exchanged cell numbers, so I decided to text her. "*Hey Donatienne how r u this morning. I am so good; I can't get last night out my head*. Her answer was immediate but typed much more formal.

"*I am good also. I had a wonderful time. I am looking forward to this evening.*" Her return text was grammatically perfect. I so, hoped that my teenage way of text-ing hadn't turned her off. I made a note to be more formal in the future. I sent her back this: "*I made reservations for two at 'Madre's Famillia.' Is seven, okay with you?*"

"*That's fine,*" she texted

"*Shall I get some wine?*"

"*Sure.*"

I'll get two, one white and one red. I'll just walk over about 6:45, and fetch you."

"OK," she texted. *"See you then."*

You cannot imagine how slow the rest of the day went for me.

At 6:35. I walked across the street to her house, and knocked on the screen door. She yelled down from somewhere upstairs, "I'll be down in a minute, just come in on the porch and make yourself comfortable. "I'm in", I yelled back. As I sat down on a small wicker rocking chair, I looked out at Colonial Avenue, through the clean, new wooden screens, I installed for her just yesterday. Colonial is a nice little street, tree lined, with well-kept bungalows mixed in with a few twin homes, typical of many of the streets in our fine community.

She walked onto the porch, bringing me out of my musing. She was her lovely self, completely in white. Nice white mid-thigh shorts with a white boat neck blouse with puffy sleeves. "Shall we go," she said.

We got there, almost on time. The restaurant was quite small, with those tables that are sized for Lilliputians. The food was excellent though. We both had fish. She, the haddock, I had the salmon. Of course, we sampled each other's meal and we managed to drink all the white, a "Santa Margarita, Pinot Grigio." For desert, we shared a cannoli. We were there no more than an hour and a half. I paid the check and as I waited for my change, I asked her, "So what would you like to do tonight?"

"How about we sit on that delightful swing again?" she said.

"I have some Bruce CDs; I'll bring them over when we get back."

So, it was, we were sitting on my porch for the second night in a row. We were now about half way through the bottle of red, a Pinot Noir that a friend had recommended to me, highlighting, that it was especially good for romantic situations.

On this night Donatienne is much more talkative. Probably the wine. I learn that she is a bleeding-heart liberal. She rarely eats meat. She would never eat veal. On and on she went, recycling, population reduction, mean spirited conservative Republicans, air pollution, the whole gamut of societal ills. She is preaching to the choir here, I am so enjoying just listening to her, this girl, who hadn't said five words to me prior to last night. I ask her if any one had ever given her a nick name.

"People occasionally want to call me Donna and I absolutely hate that. My dad though, and I've never told anyone this, used to call me Donnie"

"Would you mind if I occasionally called you Donnie." She just smiled.

"So, how about a kiss, Donnie?"

"Maybe," she said with a seductive wink. So, kiss we did. Long sensual kisses, with Bruce crooning or whatever it is he does, in the back ground. This girl is making me crazy, it's a warm evening, and I'm fighting off chills going up and down my spine. One part of my anatomy was not chilled, however, and it didn't take her long to find out.

During one long wet kiss, she ran her hand tentatively along the inside of my thigh, occasionally high enough to lightly brush against a more pertinent part. So, slight was this touch that it seemed almost accidental. Maybe it was, but I hoped it was not. For my part, I was being equally coy, the way I was running my fingers across the exposed upper portion of her breasts ever so lightly, brushing up against those always evident Ticonderoga nipples with my forearm. Our breathing is now, noticeably elevated. The teasing we put each other through was at the same time, agony and ecstasy. This being only our second time together, I reasoned that she would not want to move too fast. At least that's what I was thinking. I placed my left hand on her inner thigh and mimicked what she was doing to me.

All the while we are kissing like the movie stars do, wet…tongues…nibbled lips, altogether an unsustainable scene.

We finally came up for air. She slowly moved her head back, all the while staring at me, with those mysterious, unblinking dark stars, and said, "Too intense for me. I don't think I ever felt or acted like this on only a second date before. I hope you don't think less of me for it."

"Are you kidding? I loved every minute of it. What do you say we call it a night, just to give ourselves time to reflect on exactly what is happening here?"

"Thank you, you are so sweet and considerate."

"Let's see what tomorrow brings." I said. I walked her home.

I gave her a long, think about this, kiss, pressing my still fully erect self against her.

"See you in the morning. Sweet dreams."

"And sweet dreams to you," she said.

I turned and walked across the street.

Later as I lay in my bed, I tried to make sense of these last few days. Here I am, twenty-six, on the verge of something almost impossible to imagine. I live right across the street from what has to be one of the most sensational girls I have ever known. Intelligent, beautiful, liberal, sweet, alluring, sexy, no baggage what-so-ever and so much more, my brain hurts thinking about it. How could it be, that this angel slipped through the cracks and somehow fell into my lap? "How could it be?" I whispered to myself.

It's now day three. I have established that she is not an early bird like me. I go through my usual routines. I call about 10:30 and ask her if she would like something from Starbucks.

"Sure, I'm quite fond of the "mocha's" they serve there. She said. Would you mind having them make it, non-fat, no whip."

"Non-fat, no whip mocha, it is. I'll see you in about ten minutes."

I came back, parked my truck and walked across the street from her house. As I mounted the last step, I could see she was sitting on her porch with a grey cat on her lap. "Come in," she said.

"So, this must be Kitty" I said. She had told me a little about her cat, and now I was about to meet her.

"Say hello to Rick, Kitty" she said. Kitty just staired at me as if I was an inanimate object. I reached over to pet her, and she hissed a loud hiss that stopped me dead in my tracks.

"She's not very friendly to strangers. And she is really fixated on me. I think she believes I'm her mother. Anyway, she'll come around to accepting you eventually. She said. I sat down next to her and Kitty. She had a nice little love seat, just big enough for two, and a cat.

"Why did you name her Kitty?" I asked.

"It's kind of a long story. Let's just say I've known her since birth and we seem to have a symbiotic relationship," she said with a bright smile on her face.

I'm watching her closely, because I know a thing or two about body language from attending numerous sales seminars, I notice that she now holds eye contact with me a split second longer than would be normal. This usually means, that you're about to make the sale or they are about to get you out of their house. In this case I interpreted it to mean that this girl really liked me. I was a little worried that I might blow this whole thing if she thought I was coming on too strong. I decided to broach the subject.

"Donnie, do you mind if I ask you a question?"

"I don't know, that depends on the question I suppose." I didn't want to hear that. I was hoping for a "Yeah sure, shoot," kinda response. I now regretted having asked it. I slogged on nevertheless.

"Am I acting too forward, I mean, I've occupied a lot of your time these last few days and I - I - don't want to, you know, be a pest or anything."

"I'm glad that you brought that up, because I was worried about the same thing myself. So, I guess, to answer your question; no, I don't think of you as a pest, and I hope you don't think of me as one either."

The cat seemed to have had enough of this conversation, she plopped down and sashayed herself into the house. As I said, it was a small love seat and as she's saying this, I am only inches away from her. Instead of answering, I leaned over and kissed her. We began making out. Soon there was a little light touching just as before.

At one point, she pulled away breathlessly and said, "Let's go up to my bedroom." I could not verbally respond. I looked into those dark eyes and raised my eyebrows, trying to produce a sense of wonderment, and a <u>yes,</u> at the same time. She stood up. I pulled her close and kissed her again. There was no doubt I was up for this.

With those pesky goosebumps coming on me once again, I followed her up to her room. We stood next to her bed, and kissed yet again. Our bodies melded, my thigh pressed firmly between her legs. She made a sweet little sound as she broke away.

She backed up one step, and sat on the edge of the bed, all the while staring intently through my eyes into my soul. I stepped back a bit. I watched as she unlaced her running shoes and slipped them off. She then stood up, facing me and slowly pulled her flower printed T-shirt up and off. Her bra was practically nonexistent, the thinnest of veneers, which explained the ever-present distraction. With a slight tug and a wiggle, she peeled off the shorts. The blue polka dot bikini briefs were next, lastly, the nothing of a bra.

She stood there for my inspection. Here she was, twenty-five years old, 5'-8", 120 lbs, with runway model legs, perfect hips, neatly groomed, dark haired, mons veneris, with an impossibly flat stomach. Some things, just should not be.

I moved my eyes up. Her breasts, as I said before, were slightly larger than they should have been, in perfect proportion to each other, two miracles on earth. A leg and ass man all my life, at this moment, irreconcilably converted. In no particular order, I stripped, walked over to her, and kissed her with prurient intent. She responded in kind. Static electricity floated us down, onto her bed.

Sometimes, sex is sex. But when you really connect it can be esoteric. For the next hour and a half, we explored each other in a give and take, no holds barred fashion. No taboos, no out of bounds, all things, permission granted. We did not speak.

Orgasms for her, were easy. I lost count of those. The only thing left to be finished now, was me. I entered her, sliding into her, ever so slowly. I was being selfish now. I wanted to savor this moment. There is always only one, first time, with someone. I wanted this to be engraved in my mind forever.

The silky, tight, wetness of her was almost more than I could stand. I almost lost it in those first few seconds. Somehow, I willed myself to hold on. I was glad I did. I got into a regular rhythm. It was pure. A slow building pleasure from there, like a comet approaching the sun, for the last time. slowly beginning to glow, brighter and brighter and then that moment when you crash into the sun, a spectacular event. When I came, I actually laughed out loud. It felt that good, and so much better than it ever had before, that to laugh was a natural thing. I remained inside her for a while to bask in the afterglow. She spoke first. "Why did you laugh? I never expected that."

"I don't know for sure, happy, I guess."

We conjoined into twin fetal positions and slept like that for a time.

I don't remember who woke up first, but when we did, we spoke to each other unabashedly of our feelings about the event. We were in agreement, that something beyond special, took place here today on Colonial Ave.

For the next two months we were soul mates, side by sider's in every booth, of every restaurant, smoochin at the movies, bike rides, picnics, day trips. We were an item.

Every other Sunday, she volunteered her time at the local animal shelter. She had an interesting philosophy about this. She was an animal lover, of that there was no question. But she understood the complexities of an over populated world and she did not seem to mind that people ate meat and stuff like that. She herself would only eat chicken or fish. She drew the line at beef, especially veal, and didn't like the taste of pork or lamb. Her love of animals was mostly of the domestic variety, specifically, the poor creatures in the shelter. I ran my long run every Sunday and hung out with my buds afterwards, so this Sunday thing of hers was really not a problem. I imagined she showed up and fed and cleaned and that was her thing. I was cool with it. She asked me to go with her one Sunday, knowing that I had a calf pull and was not going to run.

I must admit I was not too keen on the idea. I imagined that I would be cleaning up dog crap all day or some such thing. I was incapable of turning her down for anything though, so I feigned excitement and went with her.

I learned a lot about her that day. She was no ordinary caregiver. Not my Donnie. She was a critter whisperer. Whether it was a raggedy cat, a mangy mutt, a guinea pig, you name it. She was in their world when she spent time with them.

We arrived at 8 AM. I followed close behind her as we entered the one- story building, no bigger than a two-car garage. The office was somewhat grimy and in need of a paint job. The walls were adorned with new and old posters of raggedy, mal-nourished cats and dogs, the better to set the scene that these little buggers needed help and adoption. Donnie introduced me to the girl at the desk.

"Pat, this is Rick, the one I told you about."

"Nice to meet you Pat," I said. "I've heard a lot about you."

"So, you are THE RICK, I take it." She said. A little embarrassed, I responded. "Well, I guess so."

"Do you know what a saint this girl is? Do you have any idea?"

"Well yeah, sure," I said.

"No, you don't, not yet anyway. This is your first time here. You will know how special she really is by the end of the day. We are both so lucky to know her."

So, I followed Donnie around and helped her on her daily routine. One by one she managed to get just about every critter out and into the fenced in area behind the building, spending quality time with each of them. They seemed to sense the innocence she possessed. They even tolerated me. At one point, I had to use the john. I excused myself. As I walked back, Pat said. "Hey Frank, did you ever hear the story of Kitty, Donatienne's cat."

"Not really. I never thought to ask her I guess." I said.

"You're gonna love this. We were sittin' here at the desk eating lunch one day, when this middle-aged woman comes in with this box that had this mommy cat, barely more than a kitten herself, with six newborn kittens, all of them tiny little things, probably only about a day old. As tiny as they were one of them was tinier yet, the runt of the litter for sure. She was not suckling, just lying there barely alive. The lady gave some excuse that she found them in the back yard, said she was in a hurry and left without a donation or anything. So anyway, Donatienne picks this little bugger up and says. "Don't you worry little one, you're going to be okay."

"She then puts her little darling back in the box and guides her little head up to one of the mommy cat's teats. She doesn't have much luck with this as, the kitten either doesn't seem know what to do, or is just too near death to care. She asked me if I still had that baby doll's bottle in the drawer. I produced it for her. She got some milk from the fridge, heated it in the micro wave in a little cup, put it in the little bottle and very gently coaxed that all but dead little thing to take a sip or two. I tell you Rick, she carried this runt with

The Smell of Vanilla Wooden Screens

here everywhere she went for the next two months. We got to calling this little miracle Donatienne's little well, Kitty. Of course, as you know, the name stuck, as I said before, she's a saint this one."

"That's amazing." I said. It's funny that she never told me that story. "

"She doesn't tell many stories, or haven't you noticed?"

"Yea, you're right, you sorta have to pry stuff like this out of her. I better get back to work."

A couple of hours later we left, after putting in close to eight hours.

✦

It was another perfect Saturday morning in late August. It's 9 a.m., early for Donnie, but here she is for the um-teenth time, on my porch swing. She's just finishing her non-fat, no whip mocha. We are headed to the beach again, just like we had the previous Saturday. When we go to the beach, we go to the one that is adjacent to Bally's Boardwalk Casino, in Atlantic City. They have a pretty good beach and a beach bar, and you can rent big umbrellas to fend off the sun.

I put the beach chairs in the rear hatch of my Mazda Tribute and we were off. I now have a couple of "Surfer" CD's. "The Best of the Beach Boys" and "Jan and Dean", I'm playing the music loud, we're singing along. Donnie has this amazing ability. She has memorized the lyrics to every song she ever heard. I've never met another person who could do this. So, as I muddle through with the lyrics, she's like a member of the band. Who wouldn't love this girl?

We enter the Atlantic City Expressway. I'm cruising along, at about eighty. I took my eyes of the road for a second just to take in the sight of her singing her heart out.

When I turned my eyes back to the road, and in the time span of 1/10th of a second, I saw something up ahead and to the left, coming across the grassy median strip that separates the south and north bound lanes. It seemed to be some kind of a sports car convertible that's terribly out of control. It hits an embankment, flips end over end, and soars into the air, heading right for us!

Not enough time…. the vision of this car up in the air like that has been forever etched into my visual cortex. There must be something like a sound cortex as well, because I can hear it still. The hideous sound it made as it crashed directly on top of us. The vision of the airborne car, the sickening cocktail of sounds, shattered glass, metal, exploding, useless airbags. How we instinctively pushed our upper torsos, sideways toward each another, the immense weight crushing us down. The loud crack of bones splintered in an instant, the amazing absence of pain, the realization and shock that something too horrible just happened.

Fighting to stay conscious, my first thoughts were of Donnie. I had to know if she was alive. Blood was now streaming into my eyes, I wanted to wipe it away but I was pinned, the roof of the car mashed me flat against the seat.

"Donnie," I called out. "Donnie, can you hear me?" I was so relieved to hear her answer me.

"Oh God, oh God," She said. I couldn't see her. But her voice was coming from somewhere behind me.

"We're going to be alright. We're going to make it, I promise." I said. In a weak and trembling voice, she answered,

"Okay"………

The next thing I remember is some kind of distant sound. I wanted to hear it clearer, but it was hard to make sense of it. I was very confused, disconnected somehow. The sound persisted. It was slowly getting clearer to me. It was musical…….

"Mare's eat oats and doe's eat oats and little lambs eat ivy." Instinctively, I started humming the tune........I heard a female voice shouting. I couldn't make sense of what she was saying. Later I find out that she said,

"OH MY GOD, HE'S BACK, THANK YOU GOD, OH THANK YOU GOD... NURSE!..NURSE!"

Someone was touching my face...blinding light. My arms were flailing away at the air, searing pain. I can't see. My eyes are open but I see nothing. I'm terrified, I try to say, "where am I?" It comes out like gibberish, can't talk. Can't hear, can't grasp what's being said. My head is pounding........

"Ricky....... Ricky........ Are you in there somewhere?".....

I could hear this, could hear it plainly. My eyes opened....to light.... not blinding light but diffused light. I could see ghostly images. I'm somewhere, and there are people here with me.... I know I'm conscious. I don't know where I am, I want to communicate, to know that I exist, but I'm under something and it's so very hard to get myself out from it. I struggled mightily to drag myself out of that fog.

"What's happened to me?" I can hear myself say..... Many voices at once,..... too hard to decipher,.... finally one, a crying voice.

"Ricky, Ricky, are you back?"

"Where," is all I can muster. My eyes are open, I'm looking directly at the person speaking.

"You're in the hospital. You've been in a terrible accident. We never thought you'd come back to us." I can see her now. It's my sister Jenna. My sister Ashley's there too, on the other side of me. They're both hovering over me. I say, "Where's Donnie?"...... silence...... "Is she here?......the accident ..... I remember ...... Where is she?".... Still nothing.

I can now see well enough to see the tears in their eyes. Ashley comes close to me and hugs me. She says, "Your Donnie didn't make it." I knew her words were true. This one cannot lie, Jenna, now bent over to hug and hold me. We wept together until I slipped back to my safe place.

They tell me I went under for another two weeks. I think back now at that time; the second time I went under. I must have fought hard to stay there, under, that is. I was alone in the room when I came back.

I didn't want to live.

The days went by, weeks, months. I went from hospital to rehab and back again, multiple surgeries, everyone so upbeat, I was now being so polite. I knew how hard they worked on my behalf. I worked hard too. They didn't know, not even the third shrink, Cheryl, the first two having bailed on me for reasons of their own, and my early incorrigibility. These days I just wanted to get home, so I could check out. I knew how I would do it, and I knew why. I killed her. No one could tell me otherwise. I killed her. I took my eyes off the road. I had no time to react. If she had never met me she would still be here. There was just no way to get around that immutable fact. My very existence caused her to vanish. The main Doc tells me I'll be home by the weekend.

I can hardly wait.

Enter Jim, the runner. I had not seen him since our conversation at Starbucks, those many months ago. I knew he had some kind of government job and that he was sometimes sent on fairly long missions. My sisters told me he was one of my most frequent visitors when I was under. I was surprised when I heard this because we were not exactly BFF's

"I guess they told you I was here to see you quite often when you were out. I'm really happy for you that you came out of it. I was hoping you would. I wanted to see you as soon as I could. May

I speak frankly to you about something?" As I said, I do not know this guy all that well.

I thought it kind of odd when I heard that he was up here so often while I was under. I remembered though, that he has this way about him that makes you feel so comfortable to be in his presence. I'm sizing him up and thinking to myself. Another diversion, I have to stay on point here, I'll humor him and play him as I do the rest of them. He begins. "Did you know I was married before?"

"Yes" I answered, "I heard something like, you were a widower or something." He now moves nearer to me. His eyes get wide.

"That's close," he said, "The truth is, like you, I am a murderer."

So blown away, by this bit of dialogue was I, that I was sure that I hadn't heard him correctly, still staring at me intently. He said, "Why do you look so surprised? I know exactly how you feel. I killed my first wife" This kind of talk is so out of character for this guy, I am speechless. He's seeing right through me. He knows....

He continued: "My first wife committed suicide. I knew she was bi-polar when I married her, but I just never got used to the extreme swings. Even though she was on her meds, she would still, on occasion, go down real deep. I was sick of it.

The night before her death I told her, it was not working out and I was thinking of leaving her. I even slept on the couch. When I got home from work the next day, I found her lying in bed, grey white, not breathing. I tried to revive her. She was so cold. She had been dead for hours. She left a note. *It's not your fault*, was all it said, but of course, to me it was all my fault. How could I have been so insensitive? How could I have thought for a moment that I didn't love her, and that I might actually leave her.

I tried not to tear up but I did. "I never knew any of this." I said.

"It's not the kind of subject that people feel comfortable speaking about. I'm not surprised you didn't know it." He paused for a moment before he continued, as if he wanted to clear his mind.

"I came here today to talk to you. About guilt and grief, for I have traveled this road. I know what you're thinking. The tears were now flowing freely down my cheeks. I had become quite good at hiding my grief but not this day, not in front of this guy. I hardly knew how to reply. I was like a piece of clear glass to this guy.

"Okay, so you know. And you know how bad I feel but do you know how it feels to be some kind of freak. Do you know what I had to endure just to be having this conversation with you? I'm sick and tired of it all. I don't want to face my future because I don't have one," again a silent moment.

"Do you want to know what I think? I think you're selfish, and weak. You have all these fine people around you, who worked so very hard to get you to this point, the rescue people who cut you from that wreck, the surgeons who spent years to learn their craft, just to be there for you. Your family and friends, who spent countless hours at your side when you were in never-never land, not knowing what would happen but hopeful, they would get you back. I think you know I'm right."

"I'm going to tell you a little story, then I'm going to leave. You'll go home tomorrow or the next day and I hope my time here today has had a little bearing on your future."

He began: "You met my second wife and kids. I love them more than anything. I remember when I first met her seven years ago, about a year after the tragedy. A friend kept telling me about this girl he knew and that she would be perfect for me. Eventually, and reluctantly I agreed to meet her. He showed me her picture, but besides that, and for all intents and purposes, it was a blind date. I told her I'd meet her at Starbucks. As it turned out we both liked grande vanilla latte's. We talked for about an hour that first time. I found out that she was a casual runner but wanted to run some races. She kept tropical fish, just as I did. We even had almost exactly the same varieties.

"She knew my story, but didn't bring it up. I was grateful for that. We started dating. Little by little, I opened up to her about my guilt and grief. She was wonderful and understanding. She told me it was okay to keep a place in my heart for Nancy. She was willing to except me with all my frailties. The rest you know is history. I am blessed for having found her.

"Nancy was not able to have kids. As you know, I now have two. My life is so different than it was, or ever could have been. I still think of Nancy almost daily and I know that if there is a heaven, she's there, and is happy for me. It could be no other way." I listened intently. I knew what he said was true.

I doubted I would ever be that lucky, but he was such a sincere guy. He gave me a glimmer of hope. I thanked him for the visit. His parting words were, "You'll see"

I left the hospital two days later. My sisters drove me home. Along the way they gave me all the assurances; that life was good and that I would be happy again. They did all they could do. They got me in the house, stayed for tea and then left. Neighbor Ed popped in just as they were leaving and brought with him, my little Maggie. I thanked him again for caring for her all these months. He kept staring at me and looking away, obviously uncomfortable with my new look. Thankfully, he stayed for only a few minutes.

It was just Maggie and me, alone in our house, as we had been so many times before. She was so happy to see me, so eager to play. She didn't know it, but I would have to learn new ways to amuse her.

I spent my days at rehab, physical therapy, occupational therapy, speech therapy. I had to learn some new tricks about driving. I had quite a few adjustments to make. Someone was thoughtful enough, to get Donnie's grandmother's phone number for me. I never had a chance to meet her. I talked to her a few of times when she was on the phone with Donnie, but that was it. My first call to her was a couple of weeks ago from the hospital. I didn't know what to expect. Would she blame me? Would she talk to me at all?

It was hard for us, a lot of reminiscing. She went on for more than an hour, filling me in about Donnie's early years. As hard as it was to hear these things, it was good for me in the long run. After all, I hadn't known her all that long.

The second weekend, after I got home, I drove up to visit with Granny Ruth, as Donnie always referred to her. As I entered the little town of Donnie's youth, I could plainly see why she was so fond of it. The quaintness of it struck me right off. Main Street, lined with prosperous little store front shops. I passed a rather prominent four-story stone building, with a sign that said Pentatonic Hotel 1889. The people on the street seemed to be in no particular hurry. It was so obvious to me that my Donnie was raised in this place. Everywhere I looked. I saw a little piece of her, everything here, slow, serene, perfect.

As I came to the edge of town, I looked for the landmark Exxon Station and made a left. I drove the two blocks to the last house on the right. Before I got out of the car I observed that the little white Cape Cod was exactly as she had said it was. Neat manicured lawn, small garden with the tulips just now in bloom. After a minute, I got up the courage and walked up to the front door and rang the bell.

This sweet little white-haired woman, looking, to me, as I expected Donnie might have looked at 72, greeted me in the doorway with a long hug. We both wept. After a few minutes, she invited me into the living room. From a remodeling sense, the interior of the house was circa 1960. Flower printed wall paper, wool rug; she even had plastic seat covers on the sofa and love seat. We sat down on the couch and had tea. She brought out the picture albums. As I perused the albums, I couldn't help but tear up. Ruth handed me some tissues. We must have gone through a half dozen albums over the next hour and a half.

The Smell of Vanilla Wooden Screens

Eventually I composed myself. Overall, it was both a sad and sweet experience for me. Certainly, Donnie's granny, loved her so. After some time, she put the albums away, and we sat there and talked. She told me that she was happy to finally meet me. And that Donnie told her on every occasion that they talked, how much she thought of me. She told me she was glad that I was such a big part of Donnie's life, and that I should never have guilt about the tragedy, that some things are meant to be. I didn't completely agree with her, but it was surely a comfort for me to hear those words.

After that heart to heart talk, I spent the next three hours hearing stories of her younger days. I learned about her dad. How they were so close. He died so young, just barely in his thirties. It was Ruth's belief that Donnie never really got over his passing. That she was somehow a little detached after that, withdrawn. That may have accounted for why it was so hard for me to get a relationship going with her.

Eventually she showed me to the room I would sleep in. It was the very room Donnie called her own when she lived here.

I hugged Donnie's pillow and sobbed most of the night.

In the morning, we went to the hotel for breakfast, after which we stopped to get some flowers and drove the short distance to the little church cemetery where Donnie was buried. One could tell it to be a fresh grave site, as the tiny blades of grass had not yet matured. They had only recently set the headstone, a typical, small piece of shiny faced, etched, granite with a slightly rounded top. I placed the flowers in front of it. I was lucky they were able to put some lilac in the arrangement, for Donnie loved the scent of them. Ruth stood next to me as I knelt down and ran my fingers over the engraved name DONATTIENE PIERCE. As I knelt there sobbing, Ruth rubbed my shoulder and sobbed with me. We stayed there a good long while, then I drove her back to her house. She gave me some pictures and souvenirs of our beautiful Donnie. I left promising to call her often and to get up to see her when I could.

On the three-hour drive back, I got to thinking about guilt. It's a complicated thing. Here I am driving with one arm trying not to think of my own loss, the arm that is, because I am here and she is not. Yet to me the loss of my arm is particularly awful. My hands and arms are my lively-hood. How will I function at work, especially at the level I'm accustomed to, I hated that drive home. I was feeling sorry for myself, and it just didn't feel right.

Time went by. My weekly visits with my orthopedic surgeon Dr. Daniels turned into monthly visits. At one of those visits, his father was in the examining room with him, a friendly and warm elderly gentleman who was now retired from family practice. He was hanging out with his son the surgeon for the day, just observing, after the introductions and some small talk. He asked me if it would be okay for him to go over my case with his dad. I told him it was okay with me. He turned to his dad and commenced.

"Rick is a walking, talking miracle of modern medical science. He was in a terrible accident. When I first saw him, it was about two hours after they extracted him from the vehicle, and air-vaced him here, to HUP (Hospital University of Pennsylvania) this is what I was confronted with: Male patient 26 in excellent health prior to the accident. He was unconscious, due to a fractured skull with a growing hematoma. The rest of the trauma was as follows: I will describe these injuries in layman's terms, so Rick doesn't think we are talking in a foreign language: first the broken bones: From top to bottom, skull, nose, jaw, left clavicle, thirteen ribs, some in more than one place, pelvic bone, crushed, something like oat meal, if you can imagine such a thing, the left arm hanging on by a sliver of a tendon and an artery. Now for the soft tissue injuries: punctured lung, as for the spleen, it was removed. One kidney, removed, extensive liver damage, since rejuvenated. This man, standing before you here, needed immediate surgery on everything. The neuro surgeon was first. He drilled a few holes in Ricks head to relieve the pressure. They gave him a boat-load of progesterone, a relatively new treatment, to try to preserve as much brain function as possible. Next, it was the general surgeon. He removed the kidney and spleen. Twelve hours into it, it was my turn. We determined that saving the arm would be a long shot, but we decided to try it. We took tissue grafts of muscle, bone and skin from various parts of Rick's body. My team and I worked six hours to reattach it. Probably our best work ever. Now mind you, we did all this work and we had no idea if Rick, would ever wake up or even live for that matter? The only blessings for Rick in those first few weeks, were that he was somewhere far away. We went through quite a few crises during Rick's recovery. The worst of which was the infection. Try as we did, we could not make it go away. I had to make the decision, or Rick would die. That surgery lasted only an hour. I needed no team to help me. I removed the arm right below the elbow as you can see."

"Do you want me to take the prosthesis off, so your dad can see what a good seamstress you are?" I quipped.

"No," he said. "But I'm glad to hear that you're getting some of your sense of humor back. The good doc probably didn't realize it, but he was almost solely responsible for my sense of humor coming back. He has this humorous but sarcastic bedside manor about him, by that I mean, he never lets you feel sorry for yourself. He was prone to saying things like "How's that stump? Let me have a look at it." One time he actually called me Stumpy. He said, "Hey Stumpy, pay attention here." as he playfully smacked me on the back of my head. He followed that up, along with a playful grin, with this little gem: "Oh Christ, I hope I didn't just send you back into that stupid coma."

I guess it's his way of dealing with these kinds of injuries for his own sake, I don't really know, but I do credit him for helping me in a whole assortment of ways, humor being the most important. The three of us talked for about ten minutes about the current state of my recovery. The elder Daniel told me that he knew of my grief and explained to me the importance of the group grief counseling I was receiving, and that I should continue with it because grief is not the kind of wound that heals by itself. He was surely right about that. Just when I thought my appointment with Doctor Daniels was over. He said, "Well, dad, should I tell him?"

"Tell me what?" I said, sensing that something was up.

"So, tell me Rick, how do you like that pincer, fake arm, we gave you there?"

"Well I can pince things with it, if that's what you're asking me." I said with equal sarcasm.

"What if I was to tell you that you just might qualify for a little number that can do a few more things than pince, as you put it."

"Let me guess? You're gonna turn me into the 6 Million Dollar Man," (referring to an old TV show about this guy that was rebuilt after a plane crash.)

"Not quite, but this thing, I'm about to tell you about probably cost about that much."

"Let's just say you've got my attention." I said trying to hide my enthusiasm, as I hated this pincer contraption.

"Well I'll just come out with it. I don't know if you know this or not but right here at the University of Penn. We happen to have the world's foremost authority in the field of robotic prosthetics. His name is Dr. Ohara. He's not Irish if that's what you're thinking, but rather Japanese. His name is pronounced more like O-hada.

Anyway, Dr. Ohara and a team of research scientists here at Penn, have been working on a Department of Defense grant to come up with a better prosthetic arm, primarily to help the many veterans returning from the two stupid wars we seem so fond of prolonging. To make a long story short, they have assembled six of these little beauties to test on six highly deserving war heroes. Unfortunately, one of them just committed suicide. That's where you come in. They have to begin testing all six of these devices two days from now or they may lose the next grant they have applied for. They have searched the entire armed services and they can't seem to be able to come up with number six.

I put in the good word for you and BINGO; I got you in the program. That is if you want to try it. So, what say you stumpy, are you game?"

"Are you telling me the thing does more than pince."

"Ricky boy, I've seen this thing, it's unbelievable. I'll tell Ohara you're in. Show up at the Orthopedic Department on the third floor of the VA Hospital at 8:00 a.m." I didn't know quite what to say. One never knows how to take Dr. Daniels, so I just said. "Okay, I'll be there."

"Good, good, he said. I'll meet you there. I've invested so much time in you that I'd like to see your face when they hook you up to this thing." I said goodbye to the good Doc and his dad and drove home.

I spent a couple of restless nights thinking all kinds of things, the usual guilt and feeling sorry for myself and now this new thing, anticipation. I was ready for something good to come my way.

Wednesday morning, I was up bright and early, Starbucks at 6:30. I said nothing about my pending trip to the VA hospital to my morning coffee group. I didn't want them asking me questions I couldn't answer.

I arrived about 7:30. I opted to leave the pincer in the car.

I went right to the Orthopedic Clinic on the third floor. I don't think I really knew what to expect. As I entered the waiting room I observed about a dozen people. Sitting together in a row against the outside wall were three men and one woman, all in their early to mid-twenties, all amputees, lefties and righties. They checked me out and nodded to me as I walked in. The guy in the first seat, a righty like me, got to his feet and offered me his hand as he said, "and then there were five. I'm Ken, 101rst Airborne, Iraq." I shook his hand and said. "I'm Rick, and I doubt I deserve to be here."

"Nonsense," he said. We all deserve to be here. You must be the civilian, right?"

"I guess you might call me that." I said.

"Well guess what, Rick? We're all civilians now." I looked around at the rest of them. They were standing, smiling, waiting to shake my hand. As soon as the hand shaking was completed, the last amputee entered the room. Ken of course said. "And then there were six." The new guys name was Abdul. I later found out that he was an Afghani soldier who was lucky enough to get himself flown over here. He was given lodging and expenses to participate in this program. He spoke only rudimentary English.

One could feel the excitement in the room. We were all hoping for a miracle or at the very least something better than the World War II issue pincer. Before we got a chance to get to know each other in walked Dr. Daniels with Dr. Ohara. Dr. Daniels gave me a big smile and a wink. Dr. Ohara spoke first, with almost perfect English.

"Good morning, I see you are all here early. That is good because I am always early, before I take you over to our lab. I want to show you a little video." He pulled a laptop out of his bag and set it up on a table He turned the thing on. I, and everyone else in the room, saw the most amazing thing.

With the voice-over of Dr. Ohara, we watched as a technician put this amazing prosthetic arm through the motions. It was made entirely of titanium, and looked remarkably like one of the arms on the Terminator. It had four fingers and an opposable thumb, all of them able to move independently of one another. The wrist part could actually do more than a real wrist, it could bend in any direction and also swivel doing a complete 360. All the while this contraption is doing this, it is also blowing off little burst of steam coming out of little pistons at the top of each exposed tendon and making this really cool popping sound.

Dr. Ohara is explaining in the video that this contraption is actually running on a rocket fuel canister that is tucked into the

The Smell of Vanilla Wooden Screens

center. He goes on to explain that this kind of power source is many times more powerful than any battery could ever be. The user of this device should expect to have about twice the strength of a normal arm. When the video ended there was simultaneous hand to stump applause from all the patients in the room. The questions began, as you can imagine. Everything from:

"Will I break someone's hand if I shake it too hard?"

"Can I pinch a baby on the cheek?" Dr. Ohara was loving all of this. It showed on his face that he was as eager to get started as we were. He spoke again before we left for the lab.

"In the coming weeks, you folks are going to work harder mentally than you ever did in your life. I have assembled a group of experts trained in the neuroscience field to teach you to make the connections again. There are sensors on the device that will be custom fitted to what's left of the nerve endings at the end of your stubs and in some cases other areas of your upper arms. I am certain that if you work hard enough you will be able to have a pretty good functioning arm in a couple of months. One more thing, right before we go into the lab, we will enter a large room where there will be about eighty reporters and dozens of TV cameras. I have given them an allotment of thirty minutes, for questions and interviews.

He showed them the same video clip he showed us. There were many questions as you can imagine. At the end of the thirty minutes he simply said, "I'm sorry that's all for now. I have important work to do, to get these brave men and women acquainted with their new futures."

We filed out with the reporters and cameras jostling to get some questions in on us. We were so eager to get started that the six of us just nodded politely and weaved our way through the crowd. We followed Dr. Ohara through the hall to the elevator. We entered. He pushed B-2. Down we went, a quick walk to through another hallway, this one with exposed pipes and electrical conduit hanging from the ceiling. We were definitely in the lowest level of the building. We came up to a door with the words "Prosthetic Development Lab, Authorized Persons Only". He put his head real close to a device next to the door. A female mechanical voice said good morning Dr. Ohara and the door opened. I found out later that the device was an iris detector.

The lab was obviously a new renovation, everything shiny in white and stainless steel. Some areas of the lab were behind glass enclosures with technicians in protective clothing. These as it turned out were germ and dust free areas where the more intricate parts of the project were assembled. He led us to a table. There on the table were six gleaming prosthetic arms, each with a name tag indicating the new owner. I got up close to mine and just looked at in awe and wonder.

It was the coolest thing I ever saw. I glanced over at Dr. Daniels and Dr. Ohara. They both had huge smiles on their faces and Dr. Daniels was looking right at me with a single tear running down his cheek.

"Let's get started." Dr. Ohara said, six technicians, one for each of us, came over to us. Dr. Ohara introduced them to us and explained that it was their job to work with us through our training, to get us to feel as natural as we can about wearing these devices. He said it was his hope that we would eventually regard our new prosthesis, as, well, like our own arms.

My trainer's name was Yar. He was a couple of years older than me and spoke with barely a hint of a Polish accent. In the weeks that followed we got to know each other very well. As it turned out, he was an orphan, just like me. He went to Girard College, here in Philly, from fourth grade through twelfth grade. He got his Masters in Robotics from Carnegie Mellon. He was currently engaged to his pregnant wife to be, Lucy. I was lucky, I guess, as he seemed to know more about this device than the other trainers. Consequently, and as time went by I became further along in my therapy than the other fine young men and women.

We had many drills we had to master, for instance, shaking hands. With the power of this thing, anyone of us could inflict some serious pain on the hand of the shaker if we wanted to. We learned to get a feel for the pressure we were using by sensing a vibrating node they attached at the top of the device that pressed against the skin right below the elbow. If the thing was buzzing at maximum, that meant you were probably breaking someone's hand. Other drills like picking up a dime or, yes, even threading a needle were even harder to master. Dr. Ohara had created this prosthesis to do just about everything.

After eight weeks of daily training we were allowed to take them home and try them out. They offered a latex like cover for the hand part of the arm. So, if you had a long sleeve shirt on the thing would be hardly noticeable. I opted to pass on it as this thing made this constant clicking and hissing racket, not to mention the vapor puffing out of it. There was no question that it functioned in most ways like a real hand but it demanded attention that was for sure. There would be no disguising it.

As we left on the last day of our training, there was more than a few tears shed, and man hugs shared. Dr. Ohara set a schedule for us to return four times a year for a two-day update and tune up. I, being the only one living close to the hospital was asked to be the group's guinea pig. I would meet with Yar once a week for minor tweaking as well as new experiments. I was more than happy to do this, so home, I went.

Maggie was the first to greet me with my new arm. She backed up a bit when I knelt to let her inspect it. As I moved my fingers in front of her she kind of tilted her head back and forth. She cautiously came closer and sniffed at it. I wiggled the fingers really fast which caused the thing to click loudly and belch out some rapid puffs of vapor. She backed up, and barked at it, as I laughed out loud. Within a few minutes she could care less about the thing. About an hour after I arrived home, my sisters and some of my good friends stopped by, and I demonstrated for them the spectacular abilities this thing had. Everyone was happy for me and I was feeling pretty okay myself.

It's been almost a year and a half now. Physically I'm about as healed as I'm going to get. I'm running again, just not as many miles. I've been in a few races and did surprisingly well. I'm definitely not as fast, but I'm not sure if the injuries or just the natural attrition of aging. As the time has gone by I have begun to see this arm as my arm. It's not so much a thing anymore.

Yar and I became so close that he asked me to be his best man at his wedding to the lovely Lucy; little Ike, their two-year-old calls me Uncle Arm. My new arm is always a big hit around kids. They haven't learned yet that it's impolite to ask someone right out, "What's that thing?" I'm always happy to demonstrate. I have a little fun with it here and there. Sometimes I'll offer it in a hand shake even though it's my left hand. It really freaks most people out. They like--don't know what to do. Offering it that way, does sort of break the ice sometimes, though.

Another six months have gone by. It's a warm, beautiful June morning. Maggie and I are sitting on my porch swing, just quietly gliding back and forth. I'm back from Starbucks, and I'm drinking a second homemade cup of Jo. I've been thinking more lately about my Donnie. It's still hard not to tear up, but I'm not as hard on myself as I once was. I have come to believe it was just a freakish thing, and freakish things can happen to anyone. It's random.

Out of the corner of my eye I see some commotion across the street, where Donnie used to live. Two renters had come and gone since the accident, I never bothered to meet them. I didn't want to go in that house ever again.

I saw a petite blonde with a short ladder. Unbelievably, she's pushing one of my previously repaired wood screens up the ladder. She was on her tippy toes, and trying to get it to fit in place. I knew that wasn't going to happen. I made the decision to walk over there and offer my assistance. As I got closer, I observed that she seemed to be mid-twenties, something like that. She had an athletic build, and surely looks good in the shorts she's wearing. She didn't see me crossing the street so I had the opportunity to size her up. I noticed she had some nasty scaring on her legs. That's nothing, I thought to myself, as I have railroad tracks running all over my torso. As I got right up to her, she was still trying to get the screen in place. She pushed a little too hard, and started falling backward. I was now close enough to do what I did next. I managed to thrust my left arm in full popping and hissing mode under her head just a split second before it would have hit the concrete. She looked a little startled to have fallen right into my arms like that. Her foot was tangled between the rungs of the ladder. I helped to extract her from this and said, "Hi! I'm your neighbor, Rick, from across the street. And who might you be?"

"I'm Beth and I guess I'm pretty lucky you happened to be right behind me, to catch me like that. How did that happen to be, by the way?" She said with a curious look on her scared face.

"I saw you from my porch, trying to get that screen to fit.

I know a thing or two about these particular screens; we have a history. You see these old porches just keep on sinking. The consequence is that the screens need a little tweaking every couple of years or so." As I'm telling her this, I'm checking her out. A pretty girl for sure, short-ish dirty blonde hair, round face, big brown eyes, with a tight scar running strait down across her left eyebrow and continuing onto her cheek. Not freakish though, just barely noticeable. She surprises me with what she says next.

"So, neighbor Rick, did you lose your arm, or is this Halloween?" For a second, I thought, does Dr. Daniels have a younger sister? I laughed out loud.

"What do you mean? This is my arm."

"Yeah, and this is my eye." With that, she cocks her finger against her thumb and whacks herself right in that pretty brown left eye of hers. It makes a loud popping sound and she doesn't even flinch.

"Glass," she says, "I'll bet you didn't know, did ya?"

I couldn't help but laugh again. She's laughing too.

"I'll tell you what," I said. "If you will allow me, I'll just go across the street and fetch my trusty carpenter's plane and we'll have these screens in place in a jiffy."

"A jiffy, you say, neighbor Rick. Now there's a word ya don't hear every day." she said still laughing. I came back with the plane and my carpenter's horses. As she watched I deftly planed those suckers just as I had done before. I climbed the ladder, and popped them in place.

"Great job, neighbor Rick. I'm impressed. How are you with wall paper?" That remark, really made me laugh. She then said: "It's hot, it's after twelve. Do you drink beer?"

"Sure," I said

"I've got some Coors Light in the fridge. Is that okay?" I paused for a second and said: "Coors light? One of my favorites."

THE END

Made in the USA
Lexington, KY
17 November 2019